'A short and beautifully written debut … Miller succeeds brilliantly [with] a pared and unadorned prose that works its effect with a minimum of fuss.' *Sunday Times*

'A sly chamber-piece of a novel … Miller offers a psychologically convincing portrait of grief, one that – like much of Conrad's own work – suggests the barrier between civilisation and the void is paper thin. An impressive debut distinguished by its spot-on period detail.'

Financial Times

'David Miller, in this debut novel, approaches the big subject of Conrad with sensible and admirable caution … Little is said in an outright manner, so we are drawn into the text, and even put to work imagining subtexts. Writing in this way is a risk but, in this case, one worth taking. And when the author gets it right, which is often, the effect is very impressive. Perhaps even close to triumphant.'

Irish Examiner

'A subtle first novel … Its unsensational account of bereavement deserves a wide audience … The restrained prose adds bite to Miller's sparing use of simile.'

Daily Telegraph

'[This] slim, quietly elegiac novel on the death of Joseph Conrad in August 1924 is compelling … Conrad's rasping final hours in his country house near Canterbury are played out o̶f̶ ... felt.' *Guardian*

'*Today* resembles a television drama ... A sparse, taut novel ... Genuinely moving' *Spectator*

'Powerful ... This is a book that through glances and small observations keenly makes real the confusion and anger that grief brings ... Miller has revealed himself as a first-class writer. *Today* is moving and simple – a great book.' *Big Issue*

'Miller's debut packs an emotional, historical punch befitting a much larger canvas.' *Daily Mirror*

'Confidence in the evoking of mood and in staging the comings and goings of its large cast, and clarity in dramatisation of themes and characterising of central players, are only the most prominent of this book's many qualities ... There is more than a hint of [Penelope] Fitzgerald's crisp classicism in the cool-water purity and freshness of Miller's prose ... he does terrific things with language, but not blindly.' *New Statesman*

'An epic in miniature, with its 160 pages of breathable prose containing 39 characters ... but he knows his characters so well that he can pare them back to a minimum and still keep them distinct in the reader's mind ... [*Today* is] a subtle and beautiful thing.'

John Self, The Asylum blog

'Miller's debut is petite in many ways ... but size is just one of the ways in which he shows restraint, an approach that helps him create a debut novel that has no spare flesh on it at all, where restraint makes those flashes of insight all the more dazzling and writing that is so precise you feel you are in the hands of a far more experienced novelist.'

William Rycroft, Just Williams Luck blog

Today

David Miller

'It was as if all the hopeful madness of the world had
broken out to bring terror upon her heart, with the
voice of the old man shouting of his trust in an
everlasting to-morrow.'

JOSEPH CONRAD

Atlantic Books
London

**FT
Pbk**

First published in Great Britain in hardback in 2011 by Atlantic Books,
an imprint of Atlantic Books Ltd.

This paperback edition published in Great Britain in 2012
by Atlantic Books.

The line from "Hinterhof" is reprinted by permission of
United Agents on behalf of James Fenton.
The line from "Congo", from *Joseph Conrad's Last Day* is reprinted
by permission of John Burnside c/o Rogers, Coleridge & White.,
20 Powis Mews, London WII IJN

1 3 5 7 9 10 8 6 4 2

A CIP catalogue record for this book is available from the British Library.

Paperback ISBN: 978 1 84887 606 4
Ebook ISBN: 978 0 85789 390 1

Printed in Great Britain by Clays Ltd, St Ives plc

Atlantic Books
An imprint of Atlantic Books Ltd
Ormond House
26–27 Boswell Street
London WCIN 3JZ

www.atlantic-books.co.uk

For my wife
Kate,

and for our sons
Freddie and Billy,
with all my love

and because of the memory of my father
Jock

'Stay near to me, and I'll stay near to you'

JAMES FENTON

'Perhaps, if we die of anything, we die
Of distance'

JOHN BURNSIDE

Today

Saturday, 2 August

LILIAN HALLOWES was an unhurried, fastidious woman in her mid-fifties who was used to doing what she had been told to do. For this reason amongst others, she was held in high regard. Few noticed her; she was shrouded from most of them by a shawl of gossip, which told all of them nothing. She was happy not to be known.

Those who really knew her would not have been surprised when she placed his notebook in her suitcase last. The act was unconscious, a professional rite. Lilian locked both catches on the case before lifting it from her bed, leaving a decreasing impression on the pale, freshly laundered cream linen of the counterpane. She then looked up to stare at the ceiling, imagining his eyes. She smiled, a vague sense of relief becoming her, her arms held up behind her head to cup the bun of her hair before she checked everything was in place, as she continued to picture his dimmed, grey-green pupils seeing the sky from her bedroom. Lilian imagined hearing one of his more withering comments about the damp patch on the ceiling corner above where she slept. He could never come to this room, or this house, with her. Instead she remembered their hours in hotels, in his agent's office, his study, the delighted time spent at his side listening to that voice.

She had woken that morning earlier than she usually did, anxious at the possibility of missing her train, but Lilian had also admitted to herself she was unusually eager for this visit. She was looking forward to seeing him again, as she always had, always would. Lilian began to feel he might almost be with her now. Having been away for over a month, she was keen to get back into their routine. They had so much to catch up on – there would be much to say: and she would write it all down. There was so much work to be done.

Lilian did not realize she had pocketed her own notebook in her cardigan until she felt it there with her writing hand. There was never any rough strife in her turning his words into anything, just the vast eternity waiting for them, a rhyme she kept alive in her head. She stood by her bed now and checked her bag again.

Lilian wrote *everything* down. She had ink, paper, pencils, ribbons and carbon paper. She had packed the typed-up replies, together with the accompanying letters, holding up each item as if for his approval.

The other things contained in her case – save stationery, weekend clothes and changes of under-wear, her wash bag and a pair of slippers – were all gifts for others: a tin of foie gras for his wife (Mrs C. enjoyed her food), some French cigarettes for 'himself', Belgian chocolates for the Vintens and the other guests and a jar of truffles for the cousins she would be staying with, all rolled tight in one of her most durable, more colourful skirts. Lilian had crammed enough for the long weekend into the dead-leaf-brown valise, knowing both that she could not include all she needed and yet she would somehow bring too much. 'You *are* an inveterate overpacker,' he had smilingly observed of her once. She could not disagree, and was particularly tickled at being found out. 'Like me,' he confessed.

Lilian had not found a book to read for the weekend, which troubled her somewhat, but she reasoned there might well be something to pick up at the station and there would always be something to borrow at the house.

3

She checked her own slim notebook again, where she jotted all her own notes, and nodded to herself – or it – ticking things off. She had not yet forgotten to buy John a gift for his birthday and planned to remedy that in Canterbury, although shopping on a Saturday was never her ideal.

There was an hour before her train. She jiggled herself into her overcoat, a dark lime tweed (an unsuccessful stab at style she had bought herself in too much haste, as a birthday present four years before) and she then slipped the notebook into its right-hand pocket, abruptly propelled to leave, to collect her matching hat, bag and umbrella, to shut the door behind her, double lock it and go.

She would not be late for a train.

Lilian, habitually over-prepared, had made the last part of this journey countless times. The ticket never took long to purchase, nor the platform to locate. What took up time was other people: the man at the wrong platform, the tourist with the wrong money, the mother with a toddling child and a suitcase shuddering at a speed which made Lilian smile at that word. The compartment was always trickier to choose because Lilian needed at least two people there with her: she avoided empty carriages.

She did not really enjoy the ride on any train and would spend most of the time looking out at the fields, at the blinkingly bright golden yellow squares of wheat, at horses pulling hay bales or men in fields, water glittering in flashes on ponds or streams; all this was glimpsed through leafy trees and, more recently, in the gutters where cars stuttered down bumpy tracks, or when the carriage would seem to be in some sly competition with a motor on a road. She knew she would think – and would try not to think – of that other carriage nineteen years ago, with its seats soaked from her brother's blood, the unspent cartridges. Her loss could never be erased: the echo of that journey resounded endlessly for her.

The dead live longer than you think, Lilian remembered someone saying, not for the first time.

Light drizzle misted the compartment windows, a change from the torrential rain of the early morning and the night before. Lilian gazed away from what view there was and instead looked ahead at the man reading in the seat opposite. He was casually dressed, in an olive-green moleskin suit, pink shirt, neat silk paisley cravat, and round wire glasses. His stupidly light overcoat lay wilted at his side. He was, perhaps, her dead brother's age. His umbrella's tip now dribbled a shivering pool of water on the compartment's floor. The man was absorbed by whatever it was he was reading and had not looked up when Lilian had entered the compartment. She thought this slightly unusual until she inwardly admitted she would have done the same.

When travelling, Lilian often distracted herself by guessing how strangers led their lives: where they worked, what they dreamt, who they loved. She had learnt this game from JC when he observed strangers reading in public. She would speculate what book it might be: was this fellow opposite her a Henty or Cotterell or Sax Rohmer enthusiast, or might his taste lean towards something more sophisticated – Stevenson perhaps, even Wells? Occasionally she would read a page over someone's shoulder and take small pride when she could identify the novel in question. She endlessly hoped to read words she had read before, perhaps even the ones she had typed down first and seen before the author.

Lilian looked out of the window at the fields, the green smudges of trees flanking the embankments as they raced by. Watching them at this speed was like seeing solid waves. From the compartment window, they rose and ebbed, from thickets and trees through to flat ground, dipping towards the Medway, the lush land flying by her side like the sea itself. Then Lilian watched the Cathedral and the Castle as the train crawled towards Rochester, slowing as it crossed the bridge from Strood.

Her silent companion opposite gently closed his book and stood uncertainly. He turned and placed the book on the seat beside him as he shrugged himself into his overcoat, his back to her as he maintained his balance against the changing movement of the train.

She recognized the book's dust jacket instantly. Lilian had noticed it in Bumpus' the other day and had been half-tempted to buy the novel then but held herself back in the hope the publishers might have sent a copy to Oswalds – she might read it there, she thought.

What happened next surprised Lilian.

The reader had picked up his hat and put it on before lifting his case from the railed rack above. He slid open the door to the carriage passage. He fumbled in his pockets for keys. He checked his fob watch, and tucked the thing back into a waistcoat pocket, its brass chain dangling. He left the compartment; he did not look back.

His book sat in front of her. Lilian took this in. Somewhere in her head she heard the words *a glimpse of truth for which you have forgotten to ask*.

Lilian was surprised that, so far, she had done nothing, said nothing. Then she leant over and briskly picked up the book, placing it beside her. She purposely looked the other way, through the greasy pane, watching the travellers on the far platform huddling for cover, heaving rain rattling the roof and streaming down the glass. Outside, puddles seemed to simmer like the surface of a stockpot. She heard the compartment door slide shut, followed by the bang of the carriage door, and then a whistle, her heart thumping as the train juddered forward. She turned her head and looked down.

The book was still there, obviously.

Lilian rarely acted badly, but she was smiling to herself now. The train was moving away from the station. She looked out onto the platform, to see the man in his overcoat and hat, clutching his case whilst attempting with difficulty to raise his umbrella in the wind. She said to herself with a throb of bewildered excitement, *I am almost a thief.*

The book had been left behind. She could not be caught. What surprised and excited Lilian more than her crime was its promise of *words*. She took the book, slipped off the jacket that had concealed bright red boards beneath, opened it and read the wonder of a first sentence:

Except for the Marabar Caves – and they are twenty miles off – the city of Chandrapore presents nothing extraordinary.

*

The invitation, when it came, had been a surprise.

John had written to Miss Hallowes from France that he would be arriving back at Oswalds that weekend for the rest of the summer holiday, and she had replied that her Bank Holiday weekend was being spent near Canterbury.

Oh well, Miss H., in that case I shall ask you to my party, he had replied. *Will you come?*

She had smiled as she read his words and shook her head, holding a hand up to the back of her neck. She could almost hear him.

I shall be with my cousins near Harbledown, and then I am due at Oswalds after the weekend holiday, she wrote in reply. *Your parents will not wish me hanging around, especially on <u>your</u> day. And my being there will only make your father think of work.*

John started his reply, *Don't be such a ...* but the sentence trailed off. He crossed it out and wrote instead,

The place will be stuffed with the usual sorts. Let's face it, they will hardly remember it is my birthday unless you are there to remind them.

Lilian could not comment on this, not knowing if she should agree with John, or deny what was true. He went on: *I'm going to ask them anyway.*

He had, which led to awkwardness.

That Thursday evening Lilian had walked down Lee High Road and took the tram down to the Black Horse and Harrow on Rushey Green. She was sipping her ginger beer in the quiet corner when the landlord called her.

The operator connected them and Lilian said to Audrey Vinten,

'I wanted to check the arrangements for next Tuesday,' shouting to the telephone.

'Mrs C. is only just home and we have yet to make plans, but we were expecting you after the holiday, for lunch then, yes?'

Lilian could hear the tone was softer than the words – had Audrey written them down?

Lilian broke in, 'John mentioned his birthday, and a party.'

'The house will be too busy that we—' Audrey was still talking loudly into her 'phone piece but there were crackles. Lilian guessed Audrey might be being overheard and Lilian knew by whom. 'This line is bad, Lilian, sorry. It's bad. I can hear *you*.'

'I can hear you too,' Lilian said.

'Mr Curle will be staying, and Borys is expected with … with … with his wife and the new baby, as well as John. You could do your usual and bed down in his room, but – he *will* be eighteen – the house will be full,' and Audrey laughed some kindly scream. That part had not been rehearsed.

So it was not a 'no' as such and though it came to much the same thing, Lilian took no offence.

Audrey filled the crackling void: 'We shall see you on the 5th,' and then, softly, so Lilian had to hold the earpiece closely to her head, 'Charley and I look forward to seeing you – you know that.'

Lilian heard the click of a lost connection. The operator confirmed the call had been finished and was there anything else she needed? Lilian did not respond. She replaced the receiver and walked away, leaving her half-filled glass on the bar, closing the door to the pub quietly behind her.

The following afternoon, just before lunch, Lilian was at the small table in her kitchen preparing a ham sandwich, reading a leader in the newspaper about the imminent anniversary of the invasion of Belgium when the second post arrived.

After she had read the letter, she gulped, knife in hand.

Dear Miss Hallowes,

John tells us you are in Canterbury over the weekend. Would you come to lunch this Sunday? It is, as you know, John's birthday the day before.

There will be seven or eight of us, plus the baby.

Perhaps we should have a party. I am only just home as Sir Robert has been up to his customary tricks.

You know the routine here.

Affectionately,

Jessie Conrad

Lilian read the letter again to check she had not been mistaken. *Affectionately.*

John would have said, suspiciously, 'Something's up,' just as he had when the War Office letter arrived announcing Borys' injuries.

Affectionately, and *Jessie*. Something *must* be up.

Lilian let go of the knife, and ate the sandwich.

When she had read the letter for the fifth time, she took the knife up again and thoughtlessly carved a peach, slicing part of her left index finger. She rarely cut herself and was surprised by the sight of blood drops on the orange fruit. She sucked the redness away and then bit its wet flesh.

The routine here meant arrive at 12.45. *Seven or eight of us, plus the baby.* That meant John, Borys, Joan, Philip, and – who else? Lilian wasn't sure she wanted to meet Philip, or his mother.

Lilian washed the peach skin from the knife blade and rinsed her plate, picturing the baby and the others who would be there. Only after pondering this for some time, after sitting for a while sucking her finger, and throwing the fleshy stone in the bin, did Lilian find paper and an envelope, pick up her pen and write in reply,

Dear Mrs Conrad,
Thank you so much for your note. Nothing in this world could prevent me from joining your celebration. I look forward to seeing you all on Sunday.
   With kindest and fond wishes to you,
      Yours sincerely,
         L. M. Hallowes

inserting the note into an envelope, folding it closed and scribbling the address. Only after reading Jessie's words for the ninth time had she walked to the Post Office with her response.

*

Thunder.

Lilian opened the carriage door and ran, scurrying for cover under the station platform's canopy like the other mice. Her suitcase seemed heavier in this rain. She imagined, fleetingly, India and monsoons, but she had never been east of Bruges or south of Capri and knew nothing of the Empire save what she had read, or been made to read. At the barrier, she handed her ticket to a dented walrus of a man wearing a bashed cap. He smiled at her and she could see that several of his teeth were missing, one of his browned front incisors accentuating that fact.

Lilian was briefly ashamed she had not reciprocated, and hid that shame in busying herself first with her bag, then her hat and umbrella.

Outside, under dripping eaves, she raised her umbrella and emerged onto Pin Hill. She was uncharacteristically flustered, time was against her. She bustled through the dampened Saturday crowds, towards the Cathedral.

Canterbury was, for her, a city of inchoate

memories: she knew it well after so many visits that it almost felt like home – yet she had never lived in the city, or anywhere nearby. Pervading her thoughts hung the Cathedral, her compass in a place she comprehended. When lost, she would look up for it, trying to glimpse Bell Harry down a narrow street. Then, almost magnetically, she would walk north, to find where she should be. That was what she had done coming out of the station. She strode towards the Cathedral along the old city walls and, taking the slope down towards the city, through Dane John, walked into a maze of streets she half-remembered before reaching the High Street, to the corner with the jewellers and Skinner's. She knew at once where she was and where she needed to go.

She settled for a moment. It had stopped pouring: now a fine drizzle held the air. Lilian closed her umbrella and looked down Mercery Lane. At the end was Christ Church Gate. On her left she passed Hunt's, the drapers and milliners, where she had bought countless Christmas gifts for her god-daughters. The bumbling crowd was insect-like, people colliding into one another, their hats knocked by umbrellas, their shoes tripping into other people's ankles. She had a five-minute walk, minimum. Lilian picked up her case to slow again outside Crow's –

where she stalled to see Forster's new novel in the window. *Did I steal a book?* No, the book had been forgotten, left behind. *I'd give it back, of course.*

Lilian moved on. A black-clad widow stormed out from Coast's, firmly placing a hand over what looked like a wig and Lilian watched her as she darted into the neighbouring store, Boots. The crowd billowed to accommodate her, and then settled back into its original form, while she stepped on the slick cobbles. She barely noticed the new memorial there, and sped on hurriedly beneath the arch into the Cathedral Precincts.

Crows fly: Lilian aimed to walk the way they flew, in as close to a straight line as she could, over hills and even in cities, where it was hardest. This, her favourite shortcut, was never that short. It took her past the West Door and the Archbishop's Palace, round the blustery corner and down to the steps into the Cloisters, the sound of pigeons cooing from the green-splattered buttresses above. This route invariably threatened crowds but, above all, it generated guilt for Lilian. She felt somehow sacrilegious, taking this short journey from or to shops yards from where St Thomas had died. It took her past the Chapter House, beyond the Dean's Stairs through to the Dark Entry and the Green Court, occasionally bumping into an adolescent schoolmaster, a clergyman, a pockmarked, red-faced scholar in pinstripes and wing collar, or a gowned chorister. She worried she might be found out. For what precisely she could have been *found out* she would not have been sure had she bothered to ask herself the question.

Within the Green Court, Lilian felt the vast calmness of space. Walking there moved her: the sudden expanse after the enclosed stone passage. She marvelled at the trees dwarfed by stone. For Lilian, from a distance, the Cathedral looked large, yet somehow small; Bell Harry tall, yet near. Perspective had evaporated. She had not been here since the erection of the war memorial by the Norman Staircase, and with that now behind her, she looked again at all that glass and stone sketched above the earth, at how much stone was there, as if for the first time.

'It *is* quite becoming,' said a sleek voice from behind her. 'Isn't it?'

Lilian started. She turned to the man who had spoken – sandy-grey hair, a thickening chin, ten or so years younger than her, his grey-blue eyes holding her with his attention. The dog collar helped her place him, a bit. He held a small leather satchel and a hat.

He said, 'You do not live here, I would guess. You are too struck by the building.'

'You are correct, sir. I do not, and I am – although I come to Canterbury often enough not to be, perhaps …' There was nothing between them, a beatless hush, then only a musical humming from him so Lilian said sharply, 'You live here.' It was a fact before being a nervous question.

'Yes, yes – I *do* – sorry. I do. Sorry, I am the, I am the new *Dean* – George Bell.' Dr Bell smiled having swallowed up his own name with surprised, insecure haste. He knelt slightly to put down the satchel, resting the hat on it, and then rose and slowly offered his hand. 'And you are *who?*'

Lilian wondered who she was as she said, 'My father and uncles were at school here, The King's School – and, often – I often work near here. I am a secretary, of sorts. Lilian Hallowes.'

With his left hand Bell fiddled with the silk ribbons on his black bib as he took her hand in his right.

'Very good to meet you, Miss Hallowes. It is good, very good.' His was a damp hand, cloying, limp.

'What I can't quite face yet is the fact that it's all *there*,' said Lilian, surprising herself with such abstract thought, her right hand now flicking demonstratively in the air towards the Cathedral. 'There – for ever. Been there for almost ever … I think I was trying to work out how heavy it is.'

Bell nodded.

He is an Anglican, she mused inwardly.

'It's much heavier than the *Titanic*, no?'

He answered, excitedly, 'Losh, yes! What a way to think of it – crikey!'

Lilian had started into something else but Bell continued.

'There was one day last November – forgive me, I hate these things,' he slid off the ribbons from round his collar, 'but I *have* to tell you this. I was *aghast* – the fog had descended *so* low, was *so* thick, I couldn't see – well, anything. Nothing. Not just Bell Harry, but I could not see a *thing*, not the Dark Entry, just – well, just—' and his arms raised themselves, his hands formed an invisible grip as if over a big ball, which he then did not describe.

'And it rattled me – having something I know so well, know as part of my landscape – it simply wasn't there. It made me think absence is sometimes so much more present than whatever we are looking at now,' he said. 'Absence so much more present,' he coughed, 'so much more present than presence.'

The man is practising material for a sermon, Lilian

19

suddenly thought, here and now, and it seemed wrong. Bell puckered his lips into a grin at her. His right hand was down and held out again to shake hers.

'A delight to welcome you here,' his hand lingered a little on her forearm. He offered an apology for interrupting her solitude and said a rushed farewell. Lilian muttered a goodbye too.

'I expect we will meet again,' he said with unwelcome certainty. 'I've rather enjoyed our little chat – heavier than the *Titanic*! – an absence so much more present than presence.'

They smiled with one another and he loudly repeated his hope they would see one another soon, and then he turned. Bell almost danced towards the Deanery, appearing to skip through the drying puddles, his left arm holding his hat and swaying in the air, his right clutching the satchel to his breast. Lilian noticed his left heel was worn much more than the right.

Amen to that, she declared to herself. The clergy always seemed to her childish, but not in a good way. *I expect we will meet again.*

The bell tolled another hour. Twelve o'clock.

Lilian walked through the Mint Yard and into Palace Street where she arrived before The King's

School shop. *CLOSED*, of course. She gazed at the squint, sloped door, her bag at her heels, the unfurled umbrella by her side, and she actually smacked her right palm against her forehead. A Saturday, in August: summer holidays. Why *should* the shop be open? She should have gone to Goulden's and just bought John a fountain pen there, or a sketchbook. It began to rain again. *I am a very dim girl*, she heard herself think.

Lilian picked up her belongings from the steps to the shop and decided she should have a cup of tea and something to eat. There was the coffee shop on Palace Street.

Having ordered, and as she stirred one spoonful of sugar into her cup of milkless Earl Grey, she found that Chapter V of 'her' new novel began

The Bridge Party was not a success.

She raised her eyes from the page as the words made her think about John's party tomorrow. Oswalds was near Bridge – the Bridge party. What sort of party would it be? She would have to carry herself with some grace before Mrs C.; Lilian told herself it could not be that bad.

She then decided she would read for an hour or

so before finding her way to Harbledown. So unbothered by the world was she – so thoroughly transported to Chandrapore – that when the egg and cress sandwich she had ordered was brought to the table, she barely acknowledged the waitress.

When Lilian paid her bill forty minutes later, her now tepid cup of tea tasted only twice, and then sipped at absent-mindedly, she had taken only minor bites from each sandwich slice.

*

Richard Curle sat in JC's study. He licked both sides of his monocle and then rubbed the glass with one of his father's old handkerchiefs whilst listening to the rain, then watching as it dribbled and streamed on the glass of the bowed windows. Forty-eight panes in all; he had counted them: sixteen, sixteen, sixteen, making forty-eight. And then again, one by one, forty-eight.

Curle was wearing slightly too many clothes: his waistcoat constrained him, the woollen socks and heavy cotton shirt were a mistake. He knew that in a lighter suit he would have felt the cold yet now it troubled him that he would soon begin to sweat. His armpits would reek. He flushed slightly at the thought others would smell him. The weather had demanded this as well as the wind-blown drive.

JC had wanted Curle to approve his choice for a new home. Vinten and he had spotted the house a week or so ago. They had selected it to move into after Jessie's recovery. The trip seemed to Curle like a return for JC – a promised homecoming – but became what Curle would later recall as the aborted drive towards Hythe. Two miles from the coast it had become apparent JC had seized up, had ceased to breathe normally, so Curle had instructed Vinten to turn back and do so speedily.

Curle had held JC's cold hand all the way back to Oswalds. He held its dead weight and glanced down. Light brown stained the inside of the index finger, the nails all gnawed and chafed, the still elegantly long fingers, their skin creased over knuckles, veins bulged with royal purple under the moles, scars and other mottling, a small wart on the side of the fourth finger. His left hand, not his writing hand. Its owner gulped at the air from the open window like water, his chest heaving, his exhausted body quivering with effort, and his hand remained lifeless in Curle's.

When they arrived back at Oswalds, Arthur Foote half-carried JC up the stairs to his bedroom while Vinten called Dr Reid. Curle and Foote had agreed not to interrupt Jessie, and only tell her what had happened once JC himself was settled. Curle dithered downstairs before returning to his own bedroom, as he would have done in any other circumstances, and had momentarily lain on the bed, not knowing what to do or where to go, looking at the polished tips of his shoes, at the blades of grass stuck damply to them by glistening rain. He swung his legs off the bed and looked around.

All seemed calm, strangely normal for a Saturday lunchtime, as if they had never gone out that morning, almost as if the clock had wound itself back to herald the breakfast they had already had together, and the chat about work, books, the days ahead.

Everything was in its place in his room, just as it had been when he had arrived the night before – the books chosen for him, set out on the chair by the dressing table, the ashtray, the matches, and the half-bottle of whisky with soda beside it. Curle walked over to the dressing table and poured himself a small nip, smelling the malt and drinking it quickly. *I had better see if they've made some sandwiches.* Curle paused at the window and looked at the clouds, seeking some lift in the weather. He put the empty glass down on the sill and looked out at the orchard. *I am here to take his place* – the thought came to him unexpectedly. He poured himself a second whisky and this time added some soda, again gazed out of the window.

Eventually, Curle went downstairs into the kitchen. Audrey and Vinten were there, talking quietly. Curle stood there and all looked glum, none of them knowing what precisely to say.

'Reid's not there,' said Foote, appearing from the study. 'He'll be back tomorrow. But they're sending another chap, Dr Baxter – he'll be here soon.'

'Right, my dear fellow,' said Curle, slightly too loudly. 'Good. I'll go upstairs and see him.'

'He's asleep, sir. His breathing's fine. Fox brought oxygen, he's wearing a mask now. He's dozed off somehow. The pain in his arm seems to have gone. Charley's with him. I've called Sneller to collect John from the station.' Curle looked up at the ceiling. Foote continued, 'Mrs C. is having her nap – she's still asleep. The doctor's sent for more equipment.' There was little for him to do, he was redundant. Foote had everything in hand.

'I'll go and sit next door then,' said Curle. 'Thank you, Arthur.'

No footsteps upstairs or downstairs, no creak, just the hard sound of silence, weighted with anxiety and anticipation. Through the kitchen door, the noise of boiling water hissing on the stove and the clock in the hall striking three, the dog yapping and then the crunch of gravel.

Thank God for that, Curle almost said. He stood and walked towards the study door. He opened it and saw it was neither John nor the supplies that Fox had called for. It was a telegraph boy on his bicycle, handing Foote a note.

Foote came to Curle in the study doorway, a telegram in his hand. Taking it, Curle moved back to JC's study where he perched on the window sill with his back to the garden and looked at the mark on the envelope – *Kensington W* – and Curle then knew, dreadfully, what this was: the world, come to pay them a visit. In Curle's experience, telegrams never brought good news. He moved round to the desk chair and sat, found the paper knife and slit open the envelope. It was from Sidney Colvin, and he read its contents with both shock and no surprise.

Foote still stood by the open door. He coughed. Curle asked him to send the boy away; there would be no return message. Curle stood again to walk from the chair to the bow window. Again, he counted the window's panes. The rain would be doing the lawn a power of good. They would find a new house and driving down Stone Street would make them feel at home again, like being back at the Pent. If both JC and Jessie were at ease in their beds upstairs again tonight, Curle might request that Audrey cook him a mushroom omelette before Borys and his family arrived.

Colvin's news had not and could not go away. Jessie, at least, would be awake by now, and might be curious as to what was going on. Curle recalled the previous afternoon when he had written part of a letter to Colvin, taking dictation from JC directly onto the telegraph sheet:

> With all my heart and soul, with all the strength of affection and admiration for her, who is about to leave this hard world, where all the happiness she could find was in your devotion, I am with you every moment of these black hours it is yours to live through.
>
> Pray kiss her hands for me in reverence and love. I hope she will give blessing thoughts to those who are dear to me, my wife and children, to whom she always was the embodiment of all that is kind and gracious and lovable on earth.

Curle took Colvin's message upstairs, saying to himself, *Pray kiss her hands.* The sky was grey through Oswalds' lower windows but, as he climbed the stairs, the view from the landing was of an afternoon bubbling up with blue.

At the top of the stairs he could have entered JC's room. He steadied himself at the door and stared at the pine floor. Curle heard strained breathing – slowly, steadily, the occasional gasp with the customary tick in the throat. He turned left and walked steadily towards Jessie's room overlooking the garden.

'Oh, Dick,' said Jessie, plumped up smartly in the chair, tea things on the table, not all of them yet touched, although a cupcake was partially eaten, its crumbs on the saucer. She read Curle's face, saw the sheet of paper in his hand. 'Is it the boys? Are they on their way? Are they safe?'

'Yes, all is safe with *them*, Jess,' Curle said, and explained – it took some time – what had happened during the journey to Hythe. 'And this, it's from Colvin. The telegraph boy came a moment ago. I am afraid to say, I'm sorry, I am … Jess – Lady Colvin died earlier this morning.'

Jessie looked away to the window, at the glass streaked with water coursed by the lightened wind.

'Oh, Frances,' was all she could say. She sat alarmingly still, Curle watching her face shimmering into differing shapes to keep itself intact. 'Poor, poor Sidney.'

'I am so sorry,' said Curle again, blinking quickly. 'I shall go and tell—'

'No, Dick,' said Jessie, 'Dick, don't. Don't tell the Boy now. Let me. Let me tell him later.'

Curle nodded and left the paper on the silver plate on the shelf by the window sill.

She said again, 'Let me.'

Foote's voice called for Curle downstairs. Maybe the telegraph boy was still waiting or perhaps Dr Baxter had finally arrived. Curle moved over to Jessie and kissed her moist forehead.

'I'll be back, Jess,' he said.

'Will you bring Borys to me when they get here,' she said, weakly.

Curle nodded.

'Leave the door open,' she said. He left her, still propped up by the pillows. She took the telegram from its torn envelope again to read Colvin's words herself.

*

Dr Baxter had arrived.

Curle and Foote accompanied the doctor upstairs to JC's bedroom, opened the door and beckoned the doctor in. The door closed. Again, Curle walked down to Jessie's bedroom. He was taken aback to see her in an armchair and not in her bed.

'Dr Baxter's with him now,' he said.

'Who's Dr Baxter?'

'A new locum. Dr Fox came to see him as well.'

Jessie gazed at Curle, clearly unable to take this in so soon after the news of death. In the dim light of the house, his hair seemed too dark to her, and his suit too green. Her bedroom still felt oddly foreign as she had been away after the operation for so many weeks. The white of her bed's counterpane appeared yellow. The carpet had a violet hue rather than its real purple and the orange on her dressing table suddenly seemed pink. What was most worrying to her was that, with clouds still smudging the horizon and rain now streaming down the glass of the windows, the sky was beginning to look blue. Colour was slipping from her.

Jessie looked to Curle's eyes, took both his hands in hers and murmured, 'He asked me if she was better. He'd heard the telegraph boy and he knew the wire came from Sidney. "How's dear Frances? Is she better?" – that's what he said.'

'What did you say, Jess?'

'I said, "Not better." You didn't tell Baxter, did you?'

Curle shook his head. Jessie closed her eyes and breathed in, sniffing a little. Curle put this down to what he thought was shock.

'I could have said, "Not better at all," or, "She'll never get better," or, "No."' Jessie smiled at him and said, 'Or I could even have told him the truth.' She had nearly relaxed. To his surprise, she smirked and asked, 'You'd never tell a novelist the truth, would you?'

Curle did not know if the accompanying noise was a giggle and decided to take it as one of her jokes.

After a decent pause, he said, with some sobriety, 'Jess, you did what you did. It could not have done him any good to hear the news.'

She lay on the bed, the sad light of this cloudy afternoon on her brow, and she heard the sound of gravel again and the dying snarl of an engine.

As he rose, Curle winked at her, saying, 'I'll go and see if that's Borys.'

Curle's heels clattered down the stairs. He heard voices – familiar, yet not those he had expected. Into view came first the 'Russian General', his waxed moustache even more fashioned than usual. Behind Percy Sneller was young John, with rain-slickened hair and his round-rimmed spectacles, wearing an oversized greatcoat that looked as if it might have once belonged to the chauffeur but which Curle presumed was probably one of his father's. Scally was bouncing round John's legs, snuffling under the coat. Sneller was carrying John's light bag.

'We've had a hell of a journey, sir,' Sneller shouted to Curle. 'Picked the lad up from the station at twelve thirty as Mister Foote requested and – know what? – bloody puncture, 'scuse my language. All that in the bloody rain. Sorry, sir. So we're a bit late – stopped at The White Horse for a bite. No need to pay me, Mister John got me lunch and I bought him his birthday treat in the taproom – eh, John?'

John looked up from nuzzling the dog. Curle could see in John's lopsided grin that he was aware that something else was happening.

'So, I'll put it here, sir,' cried Sneller, dumping the bag by the fireplace. 'Just here, sir, eh? That'll do the trick, eh? And good wishes to your father. All good wishes, yes.' Sneller turned to give John an embrace of almost Bolshevik proportion. 'And to Mrs C., eh, sir?'

John looked up at Curle and said, 'So, a happy birthday to me,' rather wanly and Curle took John's hand and held it hard, before drawing him close and then hugging him. For a while they stood, looking at the cold hall, at the suitcases.

John finally said, 'Where's Dad?'

The afternoon had already been demanding, but Curle now saw the difficulties had only just begun.

'My dear boy, he had a turn, just before lunchtime – the doctor's with him now.' Curle heard the bedroom door above them close and Foote and Dr Baxter on the landing.

John stayed put, a stranger in his own home, waiting to listen to the doctor's diagnosis.

'He likes a Scot,' Foote was saying to the doctor, 'and always loves a Scottish doctor.' He pointed at Baxter from behind his back for John's benefit, and smiled in greeting. Baxter was shuffling down the stairs, manically wrestling in his right jacket pocket with his left hand. In due course a pen appeared. Foote crossed into the study. Curle and John watched the doctor scribble on a pad, jerking his head as he wrote.

Curle had not come across anyone quite so preposterous for some time – everything about Baxter was pantomimic. The thermometer poking out of his breast pocket, the stethoscope dangling from his left trouser pocket. The heathery tweed and unimpressive tartan tie. Best of all – Curle noticed – Baxter was wearing a grey sock on his right foot, and a black and yellow diamond-patterned one on the other. Curle wondered if he would produce a golf club soon, as if he had traipsed off some nearby green before attempting the fourteenth hole.

'The patient – he seems a bit breathless,' Dr Baxter began, 'but I'd agree with Doctor … ah, Doctor … um, the previous doctor – very bad indigestion. What did he have for lunch?' He talked with a light, probably Aberdonian accent.

'Who?'

'The patient.'

'I don't think he's been poisoned, my dear chap,' said Curle, pursing his lips now. 'Besides, he ate nothing.'

'Nothing. Good. Right. Nothing at all? Gosh! Well. Well, I think, after this, ah, this attack, he should have his teeth out.'

Baxter could observe Curle's disbelief but he could not see that John was silently splitting his sides. They had not expected dentistry.

Baxter nodded wildly. 'Yes – get all of them removed, all of them. You can get very good dentures these days. Top and bottom. Saves a lot of bother later.'

Baxter was head down, packing his bag, sliding the locks as Curle heard the clock strike five. He had been about to offer the man some tea, perhaps something stronger.

'Nothing more for me to do here. On to the next. Can I, ah, wash my hands?' Foote motioned Baxter towards the wash house as the doctor grinned at them urgently.

*

When Baxter's bill had been paid – he had quietly insisted on a cheque outside in the porch as he was saying goodbye to Curle ('Might I borrow one of your cigarettes?') – and his car had driven off, Curle ushered John to the drawing room before the fire, flicking his stub into the hearth and sipping Scotch from a crystal glass. Given the hour, John had been offered a birthday glass of sherry by Audrey, and he had readily accepted.

'What *was* the point of him?' purred Curle, holding what he knew to be at least his fourth whisky of the day. 'On to the next. On to the next – *what*?' and he laughed raucously. Audrey tittered too.

'On to the next *victim*,' suggested John and there was more merriment. Curle turned at that word, interrupted by the sound of Scally yapping and a phut and gravel. Curle looked out of the window and saw a Daimler; a Daimler meant Borys.

'It's my brother,' said John.

Curle stood under the porch and watched as Borys leapt out of the car and ran from the rain to the other side of the vehicle and to his wife, Joan, coddling the baby to her. Borys was chubbier than when Curle had seen him last, moving fatly – with the air of a soon-to-be-slaughtered pig about him, as John put it to Curle later. Borys' hair was wiped back, showing the parting line. He took the infant from Joan and dashed to the house in the rain, huddling him close.

'Amazing journey,' declared Borys, handing Philip back to his mother when she arrived in the hall. 'Made it down in less than two hours, and only touched fifty once – clear run. Bit of a headache as it slowed by Blean at the end, but clear as a bell otherwise.' He shook Curle's hand. 'Hullo, Dick,' he said, nodding to Audrey and to John, 'Hullo, John. Where's Ma? Upstairs?'

Foote appeared and announced, 'Your father has asked to see you – and Philip.'

Borys looked puzzled. 'Papa up there too, eh?'

'Borys,' said Curle, 'your father – he had a turn in the car this morning, just before lunch. He's been dozing since then. The doctor's been and given the all-clear, but he's very tired. He's been so very looking forward to seeing you, all of you. But … my dear chap, your mother would like to see you first, I think.'

Borys looked at Joan with a smile on his lips if not in his eyes. Curle realized she had said nothing at all to anyone since getting out of the car, other than to burble at her baby. To Curle, she looked astonishingly young; her slightly upturned nose and pale skin were heightened by deeply reddened lips which she sucked in when she looked at you, pale blue eyes framed by long lashes. Thin wrists and long fingers, like JC's.

'Ah,' said Borys and looked nervously to his wife. 'I'd better go up then. Now.' He moved to take Philip from her. 'Does he need cleaning up again?' he said with a sniff. 'I'll go up. When you're done, just knock on the door and I can show him his grandson. Audrey will show you where to go.'

Borys turned towards the kitchen and almost began his run up the stairs before turning to Audrey and asking her quietly, 'What time's supper?'

*

While Borys was upstairs talking with his mother and then with his father, the Vintens helped Joan and the baby. John had gone to join his brother and see their father.

Curle was downstairs, reading, when John came

to see him. With some nervousness he said, 'I think we should call the doctor out again, Dick. He can barely breathe now.'

'He saw a doctor only two hours ago. And we've got that oxygen.'

'He's changed for the worse since they've been here. Borys is in with him now.' John was rubbing his hands together. 'Please. We should call.'

Curle stood up immediately and John followed him into the kitchen. Audrey Vinten was chopping parsley, their dinner nearly ready.

'Mrs Vinten,' Curle began, timidly. 'Would you go and take his pulse again, and then let me know what you think?'

Audrey put down the kitchen knife, wiped her fingers on the side of her apron and then removed it.

Curle and John stood in silence, listening to the sound of her skipping up the stairs. John had opened the door to the garden and was leaning against the cold, damp wood, examining a hinge, wondering how it worked. He suddenly felt dread, closed his eyes and waited.

When Audrey returned, Borys was behind her. Both Curle and John looked at them.

'He's having a dreadful time breathing, he needs

more oxygen. I'll ask Charley to call the doctor. Borys agrees with me.'

Curle nodded and John looked back at the floor. Audrey said, looking at Borys first, 'Shall we? I think you should all eat something now.'

*

After the dinner plates had been cleared, Curle said he was going up to see Jessie and Joan followed him upstairs, to check on the baby. Borys stood and walked from the table to the door that led to the small orchard. The sky was bruised with darkening blue, more rain on the way. He glanced behind him and John looked up.

'Jackilo,' he said, quietly, 'come outside with me.'

For the last time in his life John did as his brother told him and stood, following him. He found Borys in the garden in the light drizzle. His brother looked at him.

'Happy birthday, Jackilo.' Borys was fumbling and held out what John at first thought was only his hand. He took the proffered cigarette. 'You know how to smoke, eh?'

'I've watched Dad for long enough. And you, come to think of it.'

Borys shrugged off a small, unnecessary laugh that was not entirely there in the first place. He stood in the light from the kitchen window and John saw what his brother was, really: a little man.

'Dick says he's been writing, and Miss Hallowes might be down after the weekend. They've been considering a house near Hythe. And one up near Whitstable. The move's got to happen soon.'

John stood and listened to what he already knew. He said nothing – Borys had always needed to be the first to tell family news.

Borys took off his spectacles and meticulously wiped the raindrops off each lens as he spoke. 'He seems to have found a new place. Dick was taking him there.'

'I know. But, this – Borys. I heard from Sneller in the car down here. But Borys. He's – he's slowing down. Mama's just had the op and can't you – well – don't you see – do they really need to move now?'

'Major Bell wants them out, the lease here is up, JC wants to go, so does Mama and—'

'And Father is not here, he's in bed, having had some kind of seizure – you've seen him. There have been two doctors in the house, another on the way, a cylinder with ox—'

Borys had walked over to his brother and removed the cigarette from his lips.

'Jackilo,' he growled, his face up close to John's. 'You know *nothing*. He'll be fine. He'll rally. I was up there with Audrey, after you. He simply needs a doctor – he's not going to croak on us now.'

John noticed his brother's green eyes behind the glasses again, set deep in the flesh of his face, the pupils darting round like jiggling tadpoles in a bowl.

Borys had begun to tremble. John knew that if nothing more was said then Borys' anger would diminish as quickly as it had come. It had been like that when they were boys, even though John was younger. They might be playing, which they did only rarely, and if John were first up a tree, or quickest to sail a paper boat on the pond, Borys' face would crumble and redden and he would dash off to complain, usually to their mother. John had fallen into the habit of needling him as he did now, with a deliberate casualness.

'You know Miss H. is coming tomorrow – Mama asked her for lunch.'

'*God alive!* Was that *your* idea? It's not as if the place isn't hooching already, we'll just get the Stork down too, eh? Bloody hell, John! You know Mama seizes up when she's here, and she's just back and you ask the—'

'I said, Mama asked her …' John stopped himself.

'It was on my suggestion, yes. But Mama wrote to her. I *like* Lilian. Remember? Miss H. said no – then was formally invited – then changed her mind. So just leave it, Borys – *your* stork's landed, and so will this one.'

John thought he heard an appreciative snigger somewhere – perhaps only in his head, but still he entertained the picture of Vinten eavesdropping, or maybe Uncle Dick.

Borys left him with no answer. In silence, he walked back up to his father's room to see what was being done.

John stayed out in the drizzle and lit another cigarette from the packet Foote had left on the kitchen dresser. He watched Borys close the door and, through the glass, he saw him take Philip from Joan and disappear. Seconds later he reappeared framed by the window on the landing above with the baby on his shoulder as he went upstairs towards his father's bedroom.

John took a drag and threw the stub out, away into a hedge and beyond, and watched the orange sparks fizzle in the damp leaves.

He needed to sleep. As he closed the kitchen door behind him, he understood with a strange ease that sleep would not come quickly.

*

Nearly all the lights had been put out in the house – one dimly lit the kitchen, another lamp quivered on the landing.

Curle had played chess with John for a while. Just at the point when his second bishop was under threat and the subsequent loss of his queen imminent, John had yawned theatrically and declared quickly that it had indeed been a long day: he needed to turn in.

Curle went up to JC's bedroom and was briskly rebuffed: 'I can't have you seeing me like this.' Curle stepped back, pulling the door shut. He tripped back down towards the kitchen, cheered by the fact of JC's brusque night-time swipe.

Vinten looked at him. He asked, 'Do you want anything?'

'My dear chap – I'd love a whisky,' said Curle. Looking at Vinten and his wife, he nervously suggested that they all have a drink.

Audrey moved to the parlour.

Curle had reopened the door, leaning on the lintel where John had been half an hour before. Raindrops were not falling but dripping. Audrey had come back with a bottle of sloe gin.

'Quiet, isn't it?' said Curle.

'The slump in the hump – it always is here. There's no noise.' Sound was always muffled there, hushed as if by new fallen snow.

Curle closed the door, and walked to the stove. Standing there, he said, 'He liked silence,' then suddenly drew back from what he had imagined. Curle sat down at the kitchen table, placing his head in his hands.

Audrey slid another crystal tumbler towards him before taking one to her husband who stood by the oven.

'We better all go to bed soon,' Audrey said. 'Miss Hallowes will be here for lunch. Sneller told me he's picking her up at the Cathedral. God knows why.'

'I haven't seen her in ages,' Curle said. 'I probably know her handwriting better than I know her.'

After a while, when they had lazily exchanged words that meant little, once everything from dinner had been washed and dried by Audrey and tidied away by Curle and Vinten, Curle bade the Vintens goodnight and took the stairs up to the landing two at a time. Before entering the bathroom, he stood and listened, for too long a time, to JC and Borys chatting, about Philip, about Daimler, Borys' prospects at the firm, all peppered by choking, and then the spark of another cigarette being lit.

Once he had finished and dried his hands, Curle walked into the corridor and closed the bathroom door. He stood for a moment before heading towards Jessie's bedroom. He gently tapped on the open door to her room. He could hear her breathing.

There was no response from Jessie. Walking back to his own room past the bathroom, Curle could hear her light snoring. He was aware that the rest of the house was now again enshrouded by the rain, aware of Audrey and Charley cleaning the kitchen floor below, setting out the things for breakfast.

I'd better go to sleep, he thought to himself. *Or we'll be talking like we did last night. He should rest.* I *should rest.*

Curle listened tensely to JC's heaving, coughing sleep, and heard Borys walking back to his father's room from the other bathroom, the murmur of the cistern behind him. Curle stood and walked towards the door. He did not say, as he had countless evenings past, 'Goodnight, my friend,' but only thought the words.

In his bedroom he removed the monocle from his waistcoat and placed it by his cigarettes, then the waistcoat, his shirt, placing them on the chair by the window. He unlaced his shoes and took off his socks, then his trousers. He put the shoes on the window sill, to air them, and poured himself another little whisky.

In bed, he picked up the collection he had been rereading and for a long while he lay and watched the words on the turning pages, taking in the sense but none of the meaning until he read them again,

> In the bush somewhere; in the sea; on a blamed mountain-top for choice. At home? Yes! The world's my home; but I expect I'll die in a hospital some day. What of it? Any place is good enough, as long as I've lived,

and Curle could read no more. JC had certainly lived; he wondered whether he himself had or ever would *live*, and stared at the door for a while. By the time he looked at it again, his wristwatch showed twenty to one.

Curle switched the flickering bedside lamp off.

Sunday, 3 August

WAKING IN A HAZE of light and calm and dread, Richard Curle was rapidly aware that things had sped up as he slept. He realized his elbow was propping him up on the bed, then that he had heard a voice – Borys' voice – and as he speedily buttoned his flies, found his socks, rolled his cuffs he heard Borys calling again for someone to relieve Foote, who had been up all hours. He took a sip from the glass by the window and shuddered at the taste of diluted Scotch.

When Curle opened his bedroom door, he saw Foote standing upright, his back against the wall, his head up and eyes closed, his face pale and torn by the night. Foote looked at him, saw an eyeglass dangling from Curle's trouser pocket. Curle knew then that things were slowing down.

They both went downstairs, Foote in the clothes he had been wearing the day before, Curle following as he haphazardly attempted to tuck in the shirt he had just rushed to put on.

They spoke for a while. Foote sat at the kitchen table, sipping tea, muttering with a bare exhaustion at what had happened. He told Curle that Borys had been up with JC most of the night, talking with him. Joan had also been up with Philip, feeding the boy in the kitchen and both of them falling asleep there.

Foote inhaled.

'His breathing ... he's not good – he's been gasping all night. About the boys – about Philip – about the car company. He's *had* oxygen, not much visible use there – he's also been bloody smoking, the stupid fool.' Curle's head rose, then Foote's immediate 'Sorry' and a cough to camouflage the comment. The grandfather clock downstairs struck eight.

'He's been thinking about moving on from here and about Mrs C. – her knee, the operation. *He* should be in a bloody hospital,' Foote added with undisguised exasperation. He spread his palms down flat on the table, and his forehead followed. Curle said nothing. 'He called Borys in at six or so and asked for the nurse, so we called Dr Reid. Reid's downstairs now, just told me he was better this morning – *better.*'

'You've been up too long. You should … you should get some rest,' said Curle.

'Not now, sir,' Foote said to the table. 'It's too late.'

'Go to bed,' Curle insisted gently.

Foote raised his head. Curle saw the tears in his eyes, his streaked cheeks.

'I can't go now, sir – not while he's still with us.' Curle then saw some thing he had never noticed before in Foote: devotion.

Curle said, 'Come here.'

*

Upstairs, Audrey Vinten applied a new dressing to Mrs C.'s knee, and told Jessie that her husband's pulse had just been taken and it was good, firmer than it had been the night before. Jessie said,

'Thank the Lord,' and when Audrey had taken away the bed linen Jessie heard him shouting down the corridor to her, telling her he was better. Ten minutes later, sipping the morning tea Charley had brought her, she heard his voice again.

'Here … you!'

And there was a thump – what she came later

to refer to as *the* thump – the sound of a suitcase being dropped. Jessie was alone. Audrey had gone downstairs to rinse her bedpan.

Jessie reached for her bell – he had called it the 'Liberty' Bell – and she shook it, the peal becoming slightly hysterical, almost reaching the solo note of a scream.

By the time Foote reached his bedroom, Conrad's body was on its hands and knees: he had fallen from his chair, headfirst. Foote noticed a small smear of blood streaking the oak as he knelt and placed a palm onto the old man's back.

Jessie had stopped shaking the bell.

Foote felt the neck with his fingers for a pulse. There was nothing. Foote leant his head down, listening for breath, his nose almost touching Conrad's. There was no sign of life.

Foote stood and, to Curle standing in the doorway, seemed to come to some civilian form of attention, stiff with respect and service. Audrey had run up the stairs, a clean towel and the washed bedpan in her hands.

'Is he dead?' she said, knowing with no doubt that he was.

Foote nodded. He walked to the window. The curtains were already drawn, but Foote pulled them to again. Audrey saw Foote dry his eyes with the back of his hand. She looked down at the smudged blood on the oak boards.

The corpse was balanced on its elbows, the left hand with its fingers stretched out onto the carpet, the right bundled into a loose fist that propped up the forehead. The hair on the head had thinned. The body looked like a mantis or a cricket, oddly angular.

There was a knock on the door.

It was Dr Reid.

Audrey shook her head.

Foote turned to face the room. Reid knelt by the body and felt the back of his neck for a pulse. Curle was still in the doorway. Reid nodded up at him, and to Borys beside Curle. Curle stepped away. His back was against the wall when Audrey hurried out. Foote came after her, then Borys, then Reid and Reid closed the door. Curle looked up at Audrey's eyes.

She looked to Foote.

Curle turned to Foote. It was over.

Curle felt Foote's arms round his back and they held one another for a while.

Audrey gasped, uselessly, 'I'd better tell Mrs C.,' but the doctor said, 'No – I'll go. I've done this before.'

Reid walked along the corridor to Jessie's bedroom, and when he was there, he closed the door behind him. Jessie looked at the doctor from her bed and said, 'He is dead.'

Dr Douglas Reid nodded.

*

Several times in the night John had been woken by water – by rain, and the filling cistern in the bathroom next to him. He had been startled early by rain sheeting down on the tiles. No picnic outdoors, then. He dozed fitfully for a while and then, waking gently, he watched the light, considered the angles of the ceiling, the corners of the window ledge, the curtains billowing in the wind. He heard voices on the stairway, then suddenly silence.

John tightened the cord of his pyjamas and got up from bed. He heard his mother's bell, then Foote's unmistakable stomping up the stairs, and other short steps down the corridor. The house was creaking. More footsteps, but this time both tentative and hurried. John heard muttering, shuffling, the sounds of people trying not to make a noise. He moved to the door, which opened before there was a knock. His brother was there.

'Get dressed.' John looked at Borys. 'Your father's dead.'

The door closed.

'I know,' said John to the dressing gown dangling from the door hook. 'I know.'

He washed and dressed, clumsily buttoning his shirt and then his flies, his fingers seeming thicker than they had the night before, every action taking longer. He walked to the bathroom and, afterwards, John went to his mother's room.

He took his hands from his pockets and looked at her. She seemed changed, her face wobbling with grief, but still her eyes looked at him, intent on *him*, and he knew she was his mother. He moved towards the bed and leant down, kissed her forehead and held her, as she said nothing to him other than dire apologies, before he moved from her and sat by the fireplace.

There was nothing, no sound, simply numbness. John watched small things happen around him – a fly ambling on the carpet, Scally greedily snuffling and grunting at the gap at the bottom of the closed bedroom door, the steam from his mother's teacup – and swiftly realized he would feel like this for a while: things would happen to him before he could happen to things again.

John stood and moved to the window, fiddled with the curtains. He heard Dick's voice at the door. He moved to the fireplace again. There was nothing for him to do here – or anywhere else, for that matter. There was nothing to say and he had never had that feeling, of utter vacancy of expression. There was a strange feeling of silence, of nothing in the world, not even the rain – nothing: nothing but a vast, hushed emptiness.

The door opened again, and there was Dick. He moved to Jessie and said, 'I am so sorry, Jessie,' and she nodded and turned her face away.

Curle said to John, 'Come, and try to eat something.'

When John left, Jessie looked up at Curle and said, 'Who's going to tell *my* mother?'

*

By the time John had eaten, the kitchen had filled. Curle was on the 'phone, Reid had driven into Bridge. John spooned up his fruit and took his bowl to the sink and left it there. He realized that nobody saw him move among them, amidst their enclosed chatter. He felt suddenly too hot.

John walked into the hall and looked up the stairs, to where his father's body lay, and then he glanced out and opened the door onto the garden. It had stopped raining. He walked towards the orchard, accompanied by the sounds of swallow and thrush, starling and crow, smelling the dampness. And John felt somehow the sudden glare of snow, the blinding whiteness of iced grass, the frozen cold of a petrified hedge. Everything, to John, looked softened or melted, strands and strings of dripping ice stretched from branches and twigs. *My father is dead*, he said in his head. He said it again aloud, then surprised himself. *Mother will be dead next.*

John blinked and everything was brown and green again. He was shocked by the dimmed green dazzle of the trees, the luminous grass, and felt tears behind his eyes, but he blinked them back and went inside, to be a man.

*

John went upstairs to brush his teeth. He observed two dark figures from his bedroom window, both striding with measured hesitation towards the porch. He saw a policeman take off his hat and then he lost sight of them.

He scurried down the stairs, almost waltzing past the landing post and then stepped carefully onto the landing by his mother's room, past his own room, where Curle was staying, and then down to the half landing, beneath the window, and heard one of the policemen say to Curle, 'May I have a word with his wife?'

'I'll take you upstairs.' The sound of shoes, a door closing, a muffle of movement and then heels clicking on the stone towards the stairs. John darted back into the bathroom and collapsed into Borys who was buttoning his flies.

'What is *he* here for?'

'He's a policeman. They're outside Dada's room. Listen.'

And they did. Voices carried up the stairs.

'There are formalities …'

'Who was the last person to have seen the deceased?'

When it was not Curle, it was difficult for Borys and John to work out precisely who was talking – the voice of medicine or the law.

'What time do you think the deceased became … deceased?'

'Do you have certificates?'

'Have the next of kin been informed?'

'What was his last meal?' at which John turned to Borys and said, 'Oh God! The doctor asked the same thing.'

Borys started to snigger.

'My God, you don't think Audrey did him in with her kedgeree.'

The two young men yelped like children and shuddered in shocked mirth, gasping at the thought of it.

'Look,' they heard Curle say, 'it can't have been anything he ate. He ate nothing. We were driving, he had an attack. He's been ill, been breathless for some time. Talk to Dr Reid when he gets back. He won't be long. Or call Dr Baxter at Canterbury – actually, perhaps not Dr Baxter – call Dr Fox. There were three doctors here. And Audrey, she's a trained nurse. He's been tired for so long, but it's still a shock. A shock, but no, not a surprise.'

'We'd better go in to see the body,' said one of the policemen.

*

Curle was outside, standing by the porch, smoking now the policemen had left. Dr Reid was parking his car (Borys had earlier identified it, gleefully, as a Rover Eight) in the drive. The doctor had gone to Bridge to collect telegraph forms and certificates. When he had walked back from the car he stood by

Curle, who asked him about undertakers, and Reid replied, 'I can call Hunt's – or I'll ask Charles Lyons. I think he knows the family.'

They went inside and turned right to the study. John and Borys were already there. Reid silently completed the forms and then, looking up, explained to them what would happen next, what had to be done.

'What does a coffin cost?' asked Borys.

'Does it matter?'

'Well, we don't want to spend too much.'

'*Borys*,' John said. 'It does *not* matter.'

Borys looked up.

'Mama has to live, she will need to move, we have a child—'

'And he still has to go into a box, doesn't he?' John watched his brother fiddling with the change in his trouser pocket. 'I don't think I can talk to you about this.'

John looked at Curle so as not to meet Borys' eye and rose and walked towards the window.

'Borys,' Curle began, 'I think I can make this easier for you both. Why don't I just deal with this? Reid and I have already spoken and Eric can help us, too. Please. Both of you have other things to think about.'

'Yes,' Borys nodded. 'I do.' He walked towards the kitchen and moments later they saw him pacing into the garden. Joan was seated on the bench under the willow tree, rocking the pram. She looked up and smiled at him, patting the bench beside her. Borys sat down yards away from them.

'I'll be back. I shall call Eric then,' Curle said, standing.

Curle walked from the study towards the front door – he had left Dr Reid and John as he needed to go to the bathroom – and as he did so he saw Scally jump up again and dash towards the gate. A smartly dressed woman and a man with schoolboy hair were walking hand in hand towards Oswalds. She was holding her handbag ostentatiously before her, its slick black somehow still shining despite the cloud. Beneath her scarf, Curle saw what he instantly judged the wrong sort of red.

'Good morning!' The man greeted Curle confidently, the woman also smiling. They looked as if they had come from a new clothing catalogue – the creaseless shirt brilliantly white, the lemon-yellow tie and cream linen suit, the protruding shirt cuffs smoothly ironed – yet were too casually dressed for church. Curle thought the man might have combed his hair; she had spent a while on hers.

'I'm Jimmy du Bois, and my wife – this is Clara.' His accent was almost becomingly American.

'My name is Richard Curle,' said Curle. 'A friend of Mr Conrad. Pleased to meet you, my dear chap.'

'We're here to see over the house,' Jimmy said carelessly, his head looking up, taking it all in – the ivy, the lawn, the promise of more grass behind the house – his hands doing what an estate agent's hand would do. 'Colonel Bell's secretary said this morning was good for you,' du Bois continued. 'We've driven over from Branshaw.'

Curle hesitated, observed Clara's burgeoning disappointment. 'I'm afraid to say things have changed. It, ah, it won't be convenient for you to see the house now – there was a death last night, the—'

Clara du Bois stopped walking and she gasped, her hand held to her chest at the place where her heart could have been beating, 'Jimmy!' and her head was next to his as they whispered and, drawing apart, Jimmy said to Curle, 'Sir, I am sorry. We should go. We should not want to intrude on others' … on others' privacy.'

'I'm dreadfully sorry – you must come back: I'll see it's arranged with Colonel Bell when everything …' Curle's words petered out.

'So are we,' said du Bois, solemnly. 'We would not wish to encroach,' and there was little left to be said.

The couple turned and Curle watched their backs as they hurried up the drive before he could say anything else. He watched them walk briskly towards their car, noticing they no longer held hands.

*

Borys was with John in their father's study, waiting for Curle's return. Borys had suggested they both talk to Eric as well. He said to John, 'We'll be responsible for his affairs now, the contracts, his estate.' He was perched on his father's desk. 'The last thing he said was that he was *really* ill this time.'

John grimaced and said, 'He wasn't wrong there.'

The telephone rang rather surprisingly. John took up the hand piece and a voice crackled, 'Is Mr Conrad there?'

'Yes,' yelled John in answer. 'Which one?'

'Monsieur *Joseph* Conrad,' a French accent now apparent.

'*Oui*,' shrieked John. '*Il est ici*, he's here, upstairs – who's calling?'

'My name is Monod. I'm calling from overseas.'

'Good,' said John, beginning to giggle. '*Bien sur …*'

'I have a question—'

'I'm sure you do. *Et moi aussi.*' A beat, another pulse of time.

'Is that Mr Conrad, the *writer*?'

'No.' John recalled the way his father spoke on the telephone and knew JC would have been inhaling tobacco smoke at this point. '*Non.* I don't think I can get him for you, now,' he said. Then, '*Ce n'est pas possible,*' before he collapsed in tears, shaking with mild, hysterical laughter. Borys moved towards the desk and snatched the telephone from his brother's hand.

'Hullo,' he said. 'I'm sorry. Sorry about that. Frightfully sorry. Yes. Yes. Well, my brother, actually, yes. You see. Yes, Monsieur Monod, please stop. Please stop speaking. You see. My father is dead, he died, he's not here now, not here to talk, um, well, yes, dreadfully inconvenient for you, yes.' And with that, Borys placed the receiver down slowly.

He took one look at John, gave him a managed grin and then John's giggle broke. He looked for somewhere to sit and then, sitting, he looked again at his brother's face and sniggered with less control.

Soon both brothers were laughing endlessly, until Curle came back.

*

Lilian Hallowes had left her luggage with George, one of her 'Canterbury cousins', and took only the gifts she had unpacked, in a suitably unobtrusive brown paper bag along with her umbrella and her handbag. She had wanted to attend Holy Communion. She had telephoned Sneller and arranged for him to collect her from Christ Church Gate at 12.15 – she would have to leave during the service – so as to drive her to Bishopsbourne for lunch.

Sneller had sent one of his boys who drove the car smoothly and with care. As usual, conversation had dried up by the time he had reached third gear.

Lilian thought back to the service, to seeing the Dean again, crisp in his white vestments, the green and golden stole round his neck, his voice no longer one eating its own words, but calmly calling the congregation to prayer – 'Graft in our hearts the love of thy Name, increase in us true religion, nourish us with all goodness, and of thy great mercy keep us in the same; through Jesus Christ our Lord.'

Lilian had little belief, but she enjoyed her church. She relished the language of the prayers and loved the Bible or, at least, its words. She listened readily, first to the Epistle,

I speak after the manner of men because of the infirmity of your flesh: for as ye have yielded your members servants to uncleanness and to iniquity unto iniquity; even so now yield your members servants to righteousness unto holiness. For when ye were the servants of sin, ye were free from righteousness. What fruit had ye then in those things whereof ye are now ashamed? For the end of those things is death. But now being made free from sin, and become servants to God, ye have your fruit unto holiness, and the end everlasting life. For the wages of sin is death; but the gift of God is eternal life through Jesus Christ our Lord.

and then Lilian stood for the gospel, watching the heavy book totter in an acolyte's hands, outstretched for the Dean to read.

In those days the multitude being very great, and having nothing to eat, Jesus called his disciples unto him, and saith unto them, I have compassion on the multitude, because they have now been with me three days, and have nothing to eat. And if I send them away fasting to their own houses, they will faint by the way: for divers of them came from far. And his disciples answered him, From whence can a man satisfy these men with bread here in the wilderness? And he asked them, How many loaves have ye? And they said, Seven. And he commanded the people to sit down on the ground: and he took the seven loaves, and gave thanks, and brake, and gave to his disciples to set before them; and they did set them before the people. And they had a few small fishes: and he blessed, and commanded to set them also before them. So they did eat, and were filled: and they took up of the broken meat that was left seven baskets. And they that had eaten were about four thousand: and he sent them away.

Lilian sneaked a glance at her wristwatch, and saw it was very nearly time for her own lunch. She stood before the blessing had begun and nodded to the steward who, once Lilian Hallowes had passed him, tutted at the inability of some parishioners to 'hold on' for the entire service.

As she tiptoed towards the West Door, dodging

the stone slabs with names inscribed on them, what echoed in Lilian's ears were the words *the seven loaves and the fishes*, but also *broken meat*. You can break bread – how, frankly, do you *break* meat?

She would have corrected that.

*

There was little other traffic on the road, mercifully, given the thickening drizzle. Lilian imagined the Dean raising the host after the Sanctus as the car crunched to a stop under the trees by the gate. She still had *loaves* and *fishes* in her head. She paid Sneller's boy while still in the car and asked him to return at four o'clock. Then, with her gloved hand on the gate, cradling the bag to her chest, she watched the car drive away, up the hill. She waved it goodbye with her ungloved hand, the one that had paid the fare, and then Lilian Hallowes closed the gate and walked towards the house.

As she reached it, she smelled the wet, the moist earth and cold, the encased odour of the house. She closed the gate and walked up the drive, taking the left side so as to avoid walking across the lawn – the unobservable approach. The side door opened. Charley Vinten came towards her, across the gravel.

'Miss Hallowes – it's … it's not good,' he mumbled. He was walking with increasing speed so as to stop her.

Lilian thought: *Mrs C. The operation. An infection.* Charley's arms were suddenly around her and through her coat she felt his palms, his fingers pressing her back.

He said into her neck, 'He died,' still astonished by the fact.

They stood there under the boughs. Her handbag had been dropped onto the gravel along with the umbrella, though she still held the paper bag. She raised her own arms stiffly, to his back. All she could hear was the rain, a distant hiss. She realized she was now holding Charley up, and that they were shaking together.

'When?'

'This morning. About four hours ago.'

'The boys?'

'John's here. And Borys, with his family. Dick's here too.'

'Mrs C.?'

'In her room.' Neither had looked at the other. They drew back from one another. Lilian peered at Charley's reddened, arid eyes.

'What happened?'

Charley bent down to pick up her handbag.

'Come on,' said Charley, holding her arm. 'There won't be any lunch.'

*

The clock in the hall had just chimed one.

Curle was standing in Conrad's study, watching Borys outside. Curle heard the gravel, but he did not see Vinten and Miss Hallowes moving up to the house. It seemed odd that even in the rain the view was so vividly clear. He felt he could almost touch Borys – speak, walk, be *with* him – the glass gossamer, not solid. Curle turned from the window and walked away towards the kitchen and the garden door. As he came to the door, he collected an umbrella.

The sound of Curle's steps on the stones made Borys turn.

'Borys, can I do anything?'

Borys threw his half-smoked cigarette stub away, shaking slightly.

'Dick.' He forced a smile.

Curle began to speak: 'Borys—' Borys turned away. Curle watched him simmer and asked, 'Is all well with Joan and Philip?'

Borys was making for the stream. When he reached the bank he continued walking away from

Curle and the house, and then he stopped. He stood very still. Curle was himself under the umbrella and he realized what he had been watching was Borys being slowly drenched. He said, 'Borys, you should come—'

Whereupon something else happened.

Borys turned to Curle and, trembling, his voice slightly louder than necessary, said: 'I hate being here, you know. *We've* never had a home. *We* had here *and* there and here, *here*.'

Borys fumbled slowly in his pocket and brought out, not the packet, but a single cigarette. Lighting it seemed to calm him. Curle looked down and spotted the ash already flecked on Borys' muddied brogues.

'Did mother tell you about that day? The day we went shooting with Major Bell?'

Curle said nothing. He had heard something a while back but knew that saying less now would mean he might hear more.

'We shot pheasants. Everyone was being the country gent. But *he* wasn't a country gent, was he?' Borys took another drag at his cigarette. His blunted eyes shone at Curle behind the wire-rimmed spectacles. 'He wasn't. He wasn't an Englishman. He *wanted* to be … But, all that shooting.' He started to tremble again. 'Bell shot some rabbits – and almost bloody well shot the dog. *Shoot the dog.* Hadji brought back a rat. Even Mama wouldn't cook a rat.' Borys sank to the wet earth, shaking. 'They might eat rats on boats.' His gaze wandered up to Curle and then, nearly surprised almost as if at the sight of him, Borys strained a smile and exhaled.

'And then I ran. I just ran under that tree. Do you see it? Do you see the thing? Over there! I ran under that tree over there.' Borys pointed. 'And I just sat there, and I don't remember a bloody thing. I sat there and just shook and there was blood and mud and guns and noise and I *knew* Bell would bloody shoot me. I could see ripped skin, the bloody flesh. I was under fire. Except, I wasn't. I sat there, and felt the noise, the whole bloody noise. Knowing all I heard was damning silence – just that: silence. And then I bloody well passed out, till Hadji was licking me, his foul tongue licking me, like *I* was some bloody pheasant. So I got up and walked home. Never told JC about it.'

Curle watched him stand up and shake himself like a wet puppy. He gazed at Borys as he lit another cigarette, smeared the wet off his spectacles and became a bit more like a man again.

'He never knew about that. Lots of stuff *he* never knew about.'

Curle said, 'None of us know everything, my dear fellow.'

'*He* never knew about *that.*'

They both stood. Curle said, 'I remember him asking someone during the war: *How can we be articulate in this nightmare?*'

'Words,' Borys growled. 'More BLOODY words. It wasn't the place for being BLOODY articulate – was it, Dick?'

Curle stopped, alarmed by the sudden anger, failing to continue what he had been about to say. Borys walked over to the hedge and looked again at the expanse of land, at the ripening fields behind it. Sheep dotted the valley. Curle looked at the myriad colours, the varied shades of green that made up the slope of the broadening weald, not saying anything until Borys turned back to whisper with an air of threat, 'Was it,' as if he had not asked a question. He dropped his smouldering cigarette and lolloped back to the house, his ashen body ambling towards some collapse.

Curle remembered that he still had not yet telephoned Eric, and walked instead back to the front door.

*

As Charley shut the front door behind him, Lilian felt the damp as she leant on the wall. Charley made to take her coat, but Lilian held up her hand and said, 'I'll keep it on. I'm going to feel numb. Shall I just sit here?' motioning to the chaise longue by the fireplace.

She took off her hat and placed it on the floor as Charley walked away towards the kitchen. She could smell the fireplace, and the usual cold dampness of the place. She heard more rain, and smelled food from the kitchen. The door to the drawing room opposite was open, but she noticed the door to the study had been closed. Charley returned as Curle arrived.

'Lilian,' said Curle. 'Hullo,' he said. 'I am sorry.'

'I can't believe I'm here,' she said. 'So sudden. So soon.'

'You'd better come through,' said Vinten.

'I have to speak to Eric. Excuse me,' said Curle and he went into the study.

Lilian rose and turned towards the back door, taking in the view towards Bourne Park, but her eyes fell to the floor and she watched the back of Vinten's shoes step slowly towards the kitchen. She looked up again, towards the window on the staircase and then to the kitchen where they were all gathered. Immediately, she saw she should not really be there: that she could be an intrusion.

Charley disappeared towards the garden as Lilian looked at them all. Then she knew again that the dead live longer than you think: *he* was here, upstairs. What was left of him was there. Lilian found herself at the door of the kitchen and looked at the table and beyond. John was there, and, at the stove, Borys' wife – she was called Jane, Lilian thought, no ... *Jan, Joan, Jean* ... what *was* she called? – with the baby, Philip – she knew his name. Mrs C. must be upstairs with Borys but she was there too, in an odd way, and Lilian said, 'I'm so sorry. I'm sorry for you all. For your mother, John, Borys.'

Nobody said anything.

'John,' she said, at which she stopped and rummaged in her bag.

John rose.

Lilian remembered, as she then fumbled in the paper bag, that she in fact had no gift to give. No cufflinks. Somewhere she had the foie gras, the cigarettes and chocolate and they all seemed suddenly inappropriate. Lilian began to glow inwardly with embarrassment and wondered if she could simply pretend by handing everything over to the lanky boy.

'Oh, John,' she began a lie, 'oh, I've left yours behind, with George.' He was beside her. She brought out her arms to hold him. 'Oh, Jackilo,' she said as she hugged him hard. 'How can this be …?' whispering to the back of his head.

She moved away from him and looked at his eyes. He glanced down. Around her she felt the eyes of others and she had no more to say. She heard Curle on the telephone next door in the study. Through the wood they heard him say, 'Pinker, Eric Pinker. Yes. Put me through,' with muffled impatience. 'My name is Richard Curle. I need to speak to him now,' he enunciated angrily. 'Joseph Conrad – he has died.' It seemed as if everyone in the house stopped what they were doing at this spoken announcement of fact to an outside world, save for the sound of Joan who patted the baby's back with her palm, gently winding him, when Philip belched with comic vigour and volume.

Arthur Foote even managed an unguarded smile, which, quickly, he wiped from his face when Joan, of all of them, caught his eye.

Curle had joined them in the drawing room. Audrey had brought the bottle of sherry, some egg mayonnaise, and mustard and tongue sandwiches, and set glasses and plates on the table.

Lilian was answering Borys, 'I've been away.'

'Where were you?' Curle asked through a mouthful. 'France, wasn't it?'

'Yes,' Lilian said – although she had become Miss Hallowes – 'in Normandy, and then Paris.'

'So, quite a dull holiday, eh?' said Borys accusingly, and then, not to Lilian but to his brother, with unrestrained envy, '*You* know all about the French, don't you, eh, Jack?'

John shrugged.

Foote coughed. Water was trickling down the windowpanes. 'He told me he was going to cut your flaming head off, Miss Hallowes. He wasn't happy you weren't here.'

John relished the stunned silence: Arthur Foote had actually *said* something. John grinned. He glanced away and watched a very green aspidistra do nothing much.

'Actually,' Lilian found herself saying to fill the silence, 'I was in Paris for two days with my cousin.

He dragged me off and we actually saw Mr Liddell win that gold medal. We had tickets from a wine company. I'm not really sure why I was there – the fellows run so horridly fast you hardly see anything, but there was something marvellously moving about it, something very stirring. I …' Lilian felt herself prattling on. They were not being conversational, so she stuttered to a halt.

Borys said, 'The crowd. It whips people up.'

John flinched.

'It does—' Lilian hesitated. 'But, well …' She had a handkerchief in her hands and pulled at it nervously. 'There is something rather magnificent about that.'

The room felt still. She continued, 'Even the French were cheering Mr Liddell on.'

John winked at her.

'I think crowds should be controlled,' said Borys.

No one spoke for a while until Curle offered, 'What, even the folk who turn up at running races and cricket matches?'

'I think they should be controlled,' Borys repeated, shivering somewhat.

John yawned. 'I might now go for a walk in the rain,' he said, unexpectedly, getting to his feet. He picked something up. 'Miss Hallowes?'

They stood in the porch, not pretending to walk.

John reached into his pocket and flipped open his father's cigarette case rather clumsily. He offered it to Lilian and took a cigarette himself. He struck a match, lit his and then hers. It took several immature attempts to keep his alight.

'Was that stuff about the Olympics true?'

Lilian laughed lightly. 'Yes.' She looked at John, and he at her. 'Do you take me for a liar?'

'No. But, you must admit. *You* at the *Olympics*. Pretty lucky to get a ticket.'

They fell into silence. She looked at him and saw his life, much of which he could never know: the baby at Addison Road, the boy she had taken to the bank, the French lessons, the bus trips, the holiday in Corsica, the growing man before her, so much more his father's son than Borys would ever be.

John said, 'I was on the boat from Le Havre this time two nights ago. I watched as it cast off and stayed on deck, staring at the lights off Cap de la Hève until they'd gone. It was so calm. Just the humming of the ship. I was coming home. It was all so normal. Then the train to Waterloo, meeting Sneller.' John started coughing and said, 'I knew something was up when I met Sneller.'

Lilian Hallowes reached out and said, 'John – hold my hand.' He looked round to see if they could be seen, despite the closed door. She said, 'It seems a world away. This is now a ... a frightful shock for you.'

He nodded, the forefingers of his left hand pressed against his lips. 'For us all.' There was a calm between them.

'Much more of a shock for you. I've had my share of death, and I've reached the age when I can almost see it coming. So, I suppose, I'm not that surprised. I'd seen him slowing down. Look, John, he was tired. He was ready to go.' She looked at her cigarette. 'That doesn't make it any easier – you'll see that when you're my age. It doesn't get harder. It just never gets easier.'

John filled the silence with, 'How old were you when your father died?'

'It wasn't my father – I was thirteen, then. The shock of death came long after my father's. No: it was my brother ... my brother, Warren – my younger brother.'

Lilian turned away and felt tears. She blinked them away and glimpsed a repeating darkness.

'I'll be fine. You've ... you've lost a father, your mother a husband. I'm—'

'Will there be anything we can do?'

'John,' she said. And again, she said, 'John.'

'What?'

She threw her cigarette towards the wall. She looked at his brown eyes and said, 'Not now.'

They left the porch and walked back into the hallway. John walked on ahead. Both heard Borys, in the kitchen, say, 'I'll take the Stork to the station. She doesn't need to wait for Sneller. Then I can drive on to Cranbrook and pick up Granny and ... yes, Mama?' Borys was patting his pockets. 'Ma, do you have any money for the petrol? I don't have any readies and left my chequebook in London. I didn't stop off at the bank on Friday and didn't expect to ... You know. Didn't expect this.'

Lilian looked at John.

'So, I suppose he didn't expect he'd have to drive back on an empty tank either,' John mumbled. They walked into the kitchen and Lilian just glimpsed the muffled exasperation on John's face – and then she saw her.

'Mrs Conrad.'

Jessie was by the kitchen table, in her wheelchair.

'Miss Hallowes.'

'I am so very sorry, Mrs Conrad. So very sorry. When we were all expecting ...'

Jessie reached across the table for her handbag. As she brought out the pound note required, Lilian

79

saw Borys' lower jaw jutting out. Jessie wheeled herself over to him.

Borys said, 'Thanks, Ma.'

There was another silence.

Jessie looked up at Lilian and said, 'Thank you so much for coming.'

'It's time for me to go,' Lilian said to John, but really to them all.

Curle popped his head round the door from the pantry that led to the study. 'Miss Hallowes?' he said.

There was a knock at the front door. John ducked out of the kitchen, into the hall and then, seeing another visitor approach, announced, 'Oh God!' not only to Lilian, though he was looking at her. 'It's the bloody vicar.'

Jessie reproached him with his name.

'They must have finished lunch,' said John.

'John,' Curle said, 'would you take him into the garden and tell him we'll be with him in a moment …' He muttered, 'Miss Hallowes, Lilian – might I … might we have a word?'

Lilian stood up and followed him into the study. Curle stood in the bay with his back to the garden facing her. A moment later, behind him she could see John listening to Canon Ashton-Gwatkin. It looked as if the Rector were showing John round the garden, pointing at shrubs and the vistas beyond. Lilian moved to the fireplace. She realized that this was the first time she had been in JC's study without him there. Before, it was always she who sat in the bay, while JC stood fretting and bellowing and acting out his words, words *the great enemies of reality*, she recalled quickly, words which paid her – and his – way in the world.

'There are,' Curle seemed to be saying, 'and you don't need me to say this, there are a number of delicacies here.'

Lilian nodded.

'I'll arrange for Eric to pay for your time.'

She looked at him.

'The time lost.'

'But I've done nothing.'

'You were here to work.'

'I've not *done* any work.'

'You've been here for—'

Outside, the Rector was giving the boy a pat on the back.

'I've been here barely an hour and a half. I came for John's birthday lunch.'

'You were due—'

'It's not about *money*, Mr Curle.' She watched Curle grimace. 'I know what this family is worth, I know what I am due. So – *please*. Now is not the time, Mr Curle, *please*.'

'I'm sorry, Lilian. I'm not doing this well …' He put his hand through his hair. 'We need to look after John.' Curle saw Lilian's eyebrows rise, lightly but seriously.

'No, you're not,' she said, slowly. 'You are not doing this at all well. Because you know, you should know, we *will* look after John. *They* won't, but they'll look after *you*. But who'll look after *me*? Not the money, not the—' and then Lilian swiftly shut herself up. 'I am sorry. I am speaking out of turn here, and I know the other reason you want me here is to say that I should be going and that Borys will "give the Stork a lift" to the station. I heard him. So I shall go. Think no more of it. I shall be at the funeral, and I shall hope to see you again. And maybe you could call Sneller so his boy doesn't come back to collect me after tea. Some other day we shall have a chance to talk, once we've sidestepped any other *delicacies*.'

Lilian stood up and watched Curle's speechlessness.

'I'm not angry, Mr Curle. Just slightly shaken and very scared. So, please – I'll go now and we can speak, later perhaps. And,' she said, as her anger dissolved and became a tenderness, 'I really mean this – I've not had a chance to say it: I am very sorry for *your* loss. He loved you. I shall see myself out.'

Curle stood up as if to say something, perhaps to stop her leaving, she thought, but Lilian walked to the door and closed it without glancing back, collected her bag and umbrella from the porch and walked out from Oswalds for what she thought would be the last time.

Borys was waiting by the gate. He threw his cigarette towards the church wall, into a bush. Lilian thought he looked dreadful.

'I'm ready when you are,' she said, as perkily as possible.

'Good, good,' he said. 'Let's go!'

Borys hovered by the car as Lilian settled herself and then banged shut the door as she sat back. He moved round, tapping the bonnet, and slid himself into the seat behind the steering wheel. Soon enough the car roared into life. Borys shifted the gearstick in reverse.

Lilian briefly looked at the house again. She thought she saw John in the window above the porch. She even held up her hand, a bit like royalty, then let it drop. Foote had opened the gate. She smiled at him as he stood with his hand on the railings. She nearly waved again. She suddenly felt hurried away, realizing that she would never come here again.

They did not say much as they drove through the lanes, as the change in the sound of the engine prevented anything other than an occasional comment. Borys feigned – or perhaps he did not – that the noise meant it was too loud to try for conversation.

'East or West?' he asked.

Lilian mouthed a word back.

'I CAN'T HEAR YOU,' he yelled.

'I can hear you,' Lilian whispered, 'all too loudly', briefly relieved to be leaving them all. She thought, *I should go north.*

'Which station? East or West?'

'Whichever is easiest – I CAN GET A TAXI.'

Borys nodded back, grinning at her maniacally like a monkey in the zoo with an opened banana, having heard but understood nothing.

By this time they had slowed in traffic and were entering the city, and Borys finally attempted conversation. Their talk ranged over a series of his pre-occupations – the baby, Joan, his mother, his brother, the funeral, who did what and when and how did you learn all this?

'You never get told anything,' Lilian said. 'It just happens to you. Birth. School. Illness. Your work.

Death. Marriage. It all happens to you. Living with it all. Nobody tells you anything about how to deal with any of that.' She paused. 'It's life … You learn. Nobody tells you … tells you anything difficult.'

'I think it's quite simple,' Borys said, at her car door. 'I need to look after Mama, and I need to look after the business.' He opened the door ready to hand her his umbrella.

She stayed seated, looking vaguely serene, her bag on her lap and she stated, 'Dick and John will help, and that's what Eric's there for, to help just as his father did,' and with that Lilian stepped out of the car.

'But I need to do it,' said Borys. 'It's *what* I *am*.'

Lilian looked at Borys, his hand remaining on the bonnet, his fingers drumming there impatiently, obviously eager to motor away. She moved to him, put her bag and umbrella down on the pavement and, surprising herself – alarming him – hugged him.

'Borys,' she said, 'I've known you for so, so long and have never said a thing.'

He pulled away and looked at her, his eyes flicking to her ears, her head, beyond.

'Stop twitching!' she said.

Borys jerked, as if he had just woken, and looked at her, suddenly.

Lilian continued. 'Borys. Don't worry about *what* you are, just be *who* you are.'

He nodded and stepped back towards the Daimler. He said, 'I'd better get on to Cranbrook, pick up Granny and Flo, otherwise I won't be back before it's dark.'

Lilian nodded to him, her lips pursed, and she stood and watched him drive away till she could see the vehicle no longer. She even raised an outstretched palm to wave. Then she walked towards the cab rank by the station, and, rifling through her bag, eventually discovered her handkerchief to wipe her already drying eyes. One of the things he had said as they drove was, 'Will you be there, at the … at the funeral?'

'Where else would I be?' she replied, only now hurt by his question.

After his car drove off she sat on a bench, nearly howling.

There was no one walking in the city. A Sunday, just after three o'clock, half an hour before evensong. She wanted to eat something – a peach, some fruit, anything wet – suddenly remembering her brother Warren, beaming at her, his child's face lit with triumph when he had sliced her an apple.

That was when she began to fail to hold back more tears.

Lilian Hallowes had spent nineteen years wondering if anyone could ever have known that that grinning child would grow up one day to sit with his head back against the window of a railway carriage and hold a loaded, ten-shilling, six-chambered revolver to his right temple and pull the trigger. They had been told Warren purchased the gun that morning. The policemen had found two notes and a number of unspent cartridges beside him on those blood-saturated seats. Everything neatly by his left side, except the blood, which had, apparently, made the floor sticky. She had always thought of him as a tidy boy.

She sat on the bench and now let herself weep again, for Warren, and her mother, and her dead, unknowing father and her other brother, knowing once more what it is to lose love, weeping at her only-ness in the world.

After a while, she stood up and walked, slowly, towards the station. She could not return to Harbledown. She would call her cousins, or write later to explain. She wanted to go home. She might have missed the train, but was happy enough to wait for the next one.

*

They could see Dr Reid coming down the stairs – a man immensely untroubled by existence, Curle reflected. Doctors could attend death, or sick children, or broken flesh and somehow still just get on with their own lives. Curle thought that he could never have been a doctor.

'Was anyone else expected for tea?' Reid asked Vinten.

'Oh gosh,' Audrey said. 'She'd asked the Goodburns.'

'I'll go and tell them,' said Reid. 'Actually, I think my wife might like to meet *him*.' Reid turned to Curle. 'She's rather interested in maths.

'If you need anything else from me, let me know. Audrey has some stronger pills for Jessie – she should have some air sooner rather than later. And the undertaker should be here soon – I've left the certificate and the other paperwork in the study in an envelope marked for him. He'll do the rest. What's more, you should let him.' He put out his hand to shake Curle's and muttered a muffled goodbye, nodding to the Vintens, thanking Audrey for her help, before saying, 'I'll go and deal with the Goodburns.'

In the study the telephone started ringing. Curle knew it would be Eric Pinker, calling him back.

*

The weather had lifted, and by the time Curle had finished with Eric, and called *The Times* and Don Roberto, it had been arranged for Jessie to sit in the garden in her long chair. Curle had watched from the study as several deckchairs were brought out, and a table, and then a cloth and trays for tea things. He heard the sound of Foote and Vinten lifting Jessie down the stairs and now Audrey stood behind her chair, Joan beside her with the baby. The Rector's wife was pouring tea.

'Oh, Nancy,' said Jessie. 'Thank you. Just look at the little pickle. Joan, eh, bring me the pickle Pip.' There was strained laughter. Jessie's grin broadened. Then she noticed Curle. 'What's been happening, Dick?' she asked, holding the baby's tiny hand, cooing at him.

'The undertaker is coming, a man called Lyons. He's going to help me with the arrangements. Borys has taken Miss Hallowes to the station, and then he's off to collect your mother and sister.'

There was some idle chat, then a long conversation about Jessie's brother who had died on board a ship off the coast of South Africa during a hurricane. 'But it was actually the 'flu that took him off,' said Jessie. 'My poor mother – she's not been so alive since Frank. Her youngest dead – imagine.'

But John could not imagine. Upstairs was his father, dead, and he could not even imagine that.

Skinny, pretty Mrs Ashton-Gwatkin poured more tea and asked questions of them all – Joan struck silent by one about her wedding – and when Jessie's head had begun to nod, and her nose and mouth between them had begun, slightly, to click thickly towards a full snore, Curle suggested they all move away. Jessie was in the shade of the large pine tree on the lawn, and the sun could do her no more damage.

John glanced behind him as they walked over to the chairs set up on the lawn by Oswalds' front door. It seemed odd that she could sleep, but she was tired. He was exhausted. He looked back at her. *Never mind, Mum*, came to him from somewhere. He saw her anew not as his mother, as a woman fattened by ill health, bandaged. She seemed so remote from him.

Audrey had done as Dr Reid had instructed and rolled down the dressing to expose to the fresh air the most recent wound on Jessie's knee. From where he stood, John could see the red badge on the lint above his mother's shin, and could hear the flies already buzzing around the weeping stitches, around the gash.

*

Curle paced on the gravel outside the study, smoking. There was the undertaker who coughed behind him.

Curle turned, greeted him.

'I'm sorry for your loss, sir.'

Curle thanked him, nodding to the gravel.

'I knew your father when you were all living at Capel—'

'Ah,' Curle interrupted, holding his eye. 'Sorry. I am not his son, not Borys. I am a friend. I am Richard Curle.' He reached out his hand.

The other man's hand was cold, rough with its firm grasp. He was dressed in black, a trim waistcoat and neat, creased trousers, a white collarless shirt. A red handkerchief peeped from his trouser pocket. Curle registered the gold band on the fourth finger of his calloused left hand, and the nervous smile below a neatly trimmed moustache. His face was freckled, his eyes bright blue, kind, a warmth about him.

'Lyons, sir. Charles Lyons. Dr Reid called me here. My sister worked for Mr Conrad a while back – Nellie.'

Curle motioned to Lyons to sit with him on one of the iron benches outside the drawing-room window. He lit a cigarette.

'Sorry, sir. It's been a while since I've seen Borys and I thought you were him. But you're not. Obviously.'

'No. I thought we'd cleared that up,' said Curle, smiling as he blew rings in the still air. 'Nellie Lyons – I never knew her. She worked at – you were saying – at Capel House? I've heard Jessie mention her. Where is she now?'

'She died, sir – carried off in '19. Mr Conrad and his wife were so very kind to us then. It's why I'm here, I thought I would, well, do as I was done by. Dr Reid called Hunt's and so here I am.'

Curle looked at Lyons as he continued.

'She loved them both – she was ill latterly, but they looked after her and everything. Mr Conrad paid for the funeral and all, and gave my Ma money after, when things were tight after the war and with Jane and me working. I'll do all I can to help.'

'Mr Lyons—' said Curle.

'Please, call me Charles.'

'Charles, I *do* need your help. I shall need a word with the priest at the Catholic church – I don't know his name – and I'll need to arrange for a printer, for an order of service, and I'll need to know where we can get flowers. The family will want a short service, I should think, and it would be best if it were done quickly. I'll need to know how soon the burial can take place and I suppose I'll need to tell the family how much this will all cost.' Curle looked to Lyons. 'I've never done this, Charles.'

Curle heard him say, 'How could I think you was Borys?' Lyons was grinning broadly now, relieved at understanding his misunderstanding.

They walked to the study, talking for a further forty minutes there. Lyons made some useful decisions.

Curle strolled around the study while Lyons took notes, perching on the window sill. At one point Curle asked Lyons to wait, and Curle walked over to the tree under which Jessie was lying. She was awake, now talking to the Rector's wife, who had asked to stay with her until Mrs George and Jessie's sister arrived.

Curle said to Jessie, 'I have to interrupt,' and he wheeled Jessie away to say quietly, 'There's something I have to ask. Where did he wish to be buried?'

Jessie replied, 'That was something I did not know, and now will never know.' She coughed. 'Nancy, would you be a dear and get a fresh pot while I talk to Mr Curle?'

By the time the Rector's wife returned from the kitchen, Jessie had instructed Lyons to acquire, on her behalf, four plots, two large and two small, at the St Dunstan's Cemetery. She pleaded with Curle, 'Don't tell the kids,' not wanting either to know where she had thought to bury them.

*

After supper, John went for a walk through the house. He was trying to hold his father in his mind, attempting to place him there, then; here, now. John recalled him flicking bread pellets at supper – much to Borys' mirth – or slurping his soup and dabbing his beard with a napkin.

When everything was cleared away, John moved into the hallway and looked to where he and Curle had played chess the night before, in the alcove by the fireplace. John had often sat there, resetting the pieces, waiting for his father to come out of his study.

As evening began to fall, John understood he wanted to see the study in the glimmer for the last time. The handle to the door to his father's study turned easily, almost silently, and what surprised John most was he found there – not Curle, but Borys. The table lamp illuminating stacks of papers and books.

Borys was writing, stopping, writing, inspecting his effort, then writing again. The scratch of the fountain pen was the only audible thing in the room. It was gold, thin, the one his father always favoured.

John coughed and said, 'Hullo there,' as an indication he had walked right into the room.

Borys looked up, the faces of his spectacles like coins of white paper. 'What are you looking for?'

'Nothing, just wandering about. What are you doing?'

'Just looking at papers, thinking.'

John moved towards the desk and saw, suddenly, Miss Hallowes' tidy, thick-nibbed scrawl: sheets with underlinings, suggestions, numbers in the margin, lying amidst his father's familiar hand.

'And what are you writing?'

'Oh, taking notes, nothing much,' which John knew meant something, so he looked down at what was before Borys. It was, John discerned, even reading from upside down, his father's signature,

Joseph Conrad
Joseph Conrad
Joseph Conrad

the *h* looping onto the beginning of the next word to the top of the *C*.

'I've always liked his signature,' mumbled Borys, 'always wanted it.'

He looked up and John saw the sheen of sweat on his brother's forehead under the heat of the naked bulb. John leant over and offered Borys his handkerchief to mop his brow, and Borys took it. Then John took another fountain pen, a new-looking Sheaffer pen, gold and thin, and slipped it into his right-hand pocket.

John looked down. The *p* attached to the *h*, the *o* crossed by a line from *h* to *C* and that deep dash back, to the left of the *d*. *The hand lives on after you*, John thought, *a person lives on in their writing – a shopping list, a letter, a name etched in the front cover of a book.* The *J* almost a *T*. John noticed for the first time that his father's name only used one letter of the alphabet twice, and saw again that *C*, with its opening line harpooning the *o*. And finally he saw this was his brother's attempt at their father's signature. He breathed in.

'I'm tired,' said Borys, handing back the handkerchief.

'I'm going to bed too, Borys,' John said, starkly. 'Sleep well.'

*

Audrey had left Jessie. There was warm milk in the jug by the heated mug, a spoon, some chocolate, her powders – all left as usual, but tonight Audrey had also mentioned Reid had given her some stronger pills for pain, and for easing her sleep.

For the first time since the death of her husband, Jessie was alone. If there had been no death, tonight could have seemed the same as ever.

Jessie lay in her bed, attempting to sleep. Perhaps she would take Reid's pill. Her mother was now upstairs, her sister's heels clattering above. All these women had done after they had arrived with Borys was to cry and to fuss at her, themselves in shock and anxious for her. No tears would bring the Boy back, she had said.

Jessie contemplated the men in the house, those who had been here and not been here the night before. Borys, and Philip – not a man, of course – and Curle was still here, and John, then Vinten, and Foote was here but he was always there, and Borys, and now … now, no … no Boy.

There had been the time when they had shared a bed, then, after Borys was born, there had been three in the room. But when her knee had got bad and she could no longer move with ease, Conrad and she had shared a room, not a bed. When his breathing became worse, and Jessie could barely sleep without being woken by his hawking and spluttering, without his turning on the light at three o'clock to read or try to locate some tome from the contents of the small bookshop spread over his bed, they had moved to sleep in separate rooms. What kept her awake then were the times when, as they had last night, Curle and he would be talking till two, or when Don Roberto visited, or Aubry, and the younger man would be up and down the stairs, fetching more whisky, or emptying the ashtrays.

There was no talk tonight, only the sounds of different men creeping along the passageway, up the stairs to the bedrooms. The rain had eased, and she could hear the occasional honk from a car on the Dover Road, and then the stillness of the countryside, interrupted by the hoot of an owl. She had spent all those years with him, knew his every move, each breath, every habit. She had listened to locate him in the house, knew the hour by where he would be, or what he might be up to and now she felt only a heightened exhaustion, and little idea of the hour because time had crashed into her. She held up that notion: that time had collided with her, like a falling down. *This was always going to happen to me, he was older than me, but not yet, not so soon.*

Jessie lay in bed, frightened by the world, and looked at the ceiling. She realized that she had begun shaking under the covers, as she repeated, *I've failed him. I should have called the doctor much earlier.* And with that she thought again and again, *I didn't look after him.* She remembered his words from a month ago, when he had visited her after her last operation. He had arrived with a smile, pecked her forehead, and placed his hat on his lap. Jessie remembered talking to him and saw that he had been dozing off, sitting up a moment or two later to state with rage, 'I want you back home again, Jess, quickly,' as if he had known she had needed to be here, for this.

'I want you back home again,' she muttered to herself and to him.

Once she had dried her eyes on the sheets, she realized she had no need of the dark, that she wanted nothing of the dark. She reached for the switch to turn out the light, but the light remained in her mind's eye as she blinked quickly, like a little girl, and saw the image of the bulb, almost the filament. She pressed the light back on.

There was no need for more darkness.

When Audrey knocked apologetically on the door seven hours later and entered the room with another cup of heated milk and chocolate powder together with Jessie's medication, she was startled that Mrs C. was still asleep, and had slept with the glowing bedside lamp still on beside her.

Thursday, 7 August

JOHN KORZENIOWSKI ASSUMED he had been the first to wake.

The house surprised him. He lay in his bed, listening for the sounds of others moving around, watching the curtains barely fluttering in the morning breeze. There were things to think about, to plan. He found himself wondering what shape the gravestone would be. It would not be there for the service, but he thought about it, a rocky piece like his father's thumb. He wondered if his mother was lying in her bed, imagining what might happen that day.

Miss Hallowes had telephoned him the day before, calling from the hotel near where she lived and asking to speak to him, only to him, simply to let him know that she would be there at the church. She had arranged with Hunt's for a wreath to be sent to the cemetery, but she would be there herself too.

John had asked her what she would wear and she had looked at the telephone, standing in the small booth in the hotel, listening to the sounds of glasses being tidied behind her, her face creased in concern, and raised a hand to her hair. Gazing at the mouthpiece with her grey eyes, she said, 'I will wear what I always wear' – and he was aware of the operator's breathing on the same line – 'what I wear to all my funerals.'

John unwrapped the sheets from his body and rose, sitting on the bed. He sat and considered blankly the words *all my funerals*. He had never been to a funeral. *I am going to see my father buried*, he said to himself, and the phrase would keep echoing in his head, in variations: *I am going to bury my father. My father is to be buried. I will be there when my father is buried.* All ways of saying, *My father is dead*, without saying it. He would go to more funerals: his mother's, perhaps his brother's. Curle's. He might get married, and have to attend his own wife's funeral, or even their children's if he ever became a father, like his brother. John felt the calm of this first funeral, the beginning of some storm that would not end. He found his glasses.

He looked out at the orchard, the garden, the park. He could see swallows and, out of the blue, a kite swooping down from on high, diving deftly for the kill. The blueness of the sky had that early-morning hazy whiteness which promised a blazing afternoon. No wind, by the looks of it, just the threat of heat.

He heard Scally bark. The evening before, he had been about to take the dog out when his mother had called him as she had done three times a day every day since his father's coffin had arrived on Tuesday. One time she said to him, shaking, 'I'm so *sorry*,' and again, 'I'm *so* sorry, Jackilo.' John was arrested by the sudden thought that *she* had failed *him*.

'I should have been there,' she said aloud. 'What else could I have done? Could I have done something for him? But I did all I could.'

'You did everything, Mama.'

'Jackilo,' she had called from her chair in the hall. 'Can we?'

John had walked over to the chaise longue where his mother was gazing at the front door, took her hand and then, holding her up, walked with her to the darkened drawing room opposite. There were four steps and it took them several attempts to get there, Jessie squealing in pain, wincing in agony.

That afternoon she said to John dreamily, 'He didn't even die in his own bed.'

They had sat and talked about Lady Colvin and when her funeral was to be, and then their conversation moved to others who had died, to her youngest brother, his Uncle Frank, a man John hardly knew and barely recalled.

'He's buried there, in South Africa; London, East London, it's called. I'll never see his grave.' Jessie looked at her son and said, 'You might,' with an encouraging smile that seemed to John like a push into open waters.

Mother and son now stood in the drawing room, with nothing to say. The silence between them said everything. There was little light. There was the chink of crockery from the kitchen. The opened coffin had quietly appalled John. What lay there was recognizably his father, strangely swaddled in white given that in life he had almost always worn black. Curle had said he looked glorious, resplendent in death.

Now his father's face was blotched by a browning purple, the beard on his chin almost indecent. He looked like his father yet was not his father and this was what he found hardest to understand with every visit he and his mother made to the corpse. There was nothing there. There was sagging skin and hair, the something that used to be there, but even then – where was the soul? John wanted to prod the flesh and see if there *was* anything there. Had there *been* a soul? When he had kissed the forehead of what had once been his father the flesh had been cold and dead. John felt no loss, simply absence, shapeless, soundless nothing. By the last time, all he could do was hold his mother up and look blankly at the wall above the recently sealed coffin. Now, there was nothing even to see.

Jessie's fingers pressed on John's forearm. She bowed and made to move towards the door. Once they were out, and the door had been closed, Jessie made her way back to the chaise longue by the fireplace.

John said, 'Scally wants a walk,' and he had taken his leave of his mother that way, duty to a dog giving him a space to breathe once more.

*

John wore the clothes he had the day before. He would change after breakfast. He wanted to get downstairs and eat before anyone else, so he could clear his mind and prepare himself for the day somehow. He put on neither socks nor shoes and walked quietly down the corridor, past his father's room. When he was downstairs he nipped round to the garden door and turned left, to the lavatory.

He was buttoning himself up when he saw Curle, in his pyjamas, in the garden. Curle had heard the water gurgling in the drain and looked over in his direction. He smiled and, through the window, said warmly, 'Good morning.'

John felt a sudden disappointment that he was not going to be alone as he had hoped, but was also struck by how good it was that Curle was there, doing what he had always done. John opened the door to the garden.

'Thought there might be something here,' Curle said. The garden was fresh, lush, basking in the after-dawn. It smelled of green. He looked down the orchard to the yew hedge, closing the door behind him, his palm still on the handle, the grass all of a sudden shockingly there between his toes. In the garden he saw runner beans and their odd flowers beside them, like starfish dried in the sun, only thinner. *My father is to be buried this afternoon.*

'Slightly optimistic of me.' Curle held up a rotting apple and a bird-pecked carrot in one hand.

John chuckled gently. 'Audrey's squirrel shit, then?'

'No, I've done better than that,' and, chucking

both apple and courgette over the hedge behind him, Curle bent down and raised a trug with peaches and nectarines, strawberries and apples. 'Enough for you and me, at least.'

As they stood in the kitchen – Curle washing then drying the fruit, John chopping the skin and flesh – John recalled days in his school holidays, when he was too young and never held the knife, only the towel. Curle had always said that the only way to enjoy fruit was to pick it and eat it while it was still warm from the morning sun. Curle mixed the cut fruits with yoghurt and crushed nuts in a bowl.

John finished making tea. Drying his hands, he spotted three ants making their way to the tap.

'Not precisely your father's idea of a breakfast,' Curle said, his lips pursed. He discovered a serving spoon by the sink and dolloped some of his mixture onto a plate for John, then for himself. 'Audrey's up with your mum. No sign of Borys or Joan. I heard the baby in the night, but it's all a bit – all a bit quiet.'

'I've never done this, Dick,' said John after two mouthfuls. He could still smell the soap on his hands. 'What am I meant to do? Am I meant to *do* anything?'

Curle swallowed. 'None of us have, John. You are burying your father, I'm there watching a dear friend, a great writer …' Curle stopped. He sipped some apple juice. He took a deep breath, his eyes closed, his nose suddenly snapped back like Scally's, his neck stretched. He said, 'Be there for your mother, and be there for Borys and …'

Curle stopped again. He looked at John and raised his glass as though to toast him, watching this lanky young man through burgeoning tears.

John looked at him and knew then that Curle was the next best thing he had to a brother. Both were struggling to be men.

Curle smiled peaceably, glugged down the rest of the juice and then rose and came behind him, resting both his hands on John's shoulders. 'Be yourself, John. It's all you've ever done and all you should do. All we can be.'

Scally was hovering by the legs of the table, his tail wagging with almost comic speed, like an overwound miniature metronome. Curle bent to attempt to feed him a slice of pear, but the dog would only lick the taste off his fingers.

Curle continued, 'That's all I can say, dear fellow. You'll know what to do, how to be. And don't be afraid to cry. I can't – you can.'

Curle went over to the sink to rinse his plate and wash his hands. He looked at John and did not then pretend to dry his eyes. 'I'm going to go and buff my shoes in the garden. Come and join me – when you want to.'

John stood still by the kitchen table for a while, and then stood, mindlessly tidying the rest of their breakfast things for Audrey. When he opened the door to the store cupboard to replace the butter, he looked inside, and walked towards the shelves. He touched a jar and looked at the wooden shelf. There, in his father's hand, he saw a label stating *Redcurrant Jelly, '22* and in that instant John felt his eyes begin to water again, an involuntary thing, and his whole body seemed as though it had been sliced, and shredded, cut down.

*

There were the usual empty pleasantries when their uncles arrived, most of the talk directed by Borys, asking about what roads they had journeyed down, which turnings they had taken, how their cars had performed.

John said to Uncle Albert, 'How are Belle and Enid?'

'Very good of you to ask, my boy, very good. They're very well and send you both love and best wishes at this ... on this ... at this time.'

'What's Enid up to?' John wondered aloud.

'Typewriting – very promising opportunities at the Post Office for her.'

'And the bowling?'

Albert George looked mildly surprised but his mouth broke into a gentle smile. He gave John a conspiratorial look. 'Better than her typing,' and they laughed.

'And Brendon?' said John to his other uncle, Walter.

'To tell you the truth,' Walter growled, 'he looks like an angel and behaves like the devil. Soon as the army want 'im, they can have 'im.' John recalled a smiling boy of seven or so, with his strawberry blonde hair and a face peppered with freckles, burning bright blue eyes, and perfect baby teeth.

'He must be eleven—'

'Twelve,' said Walter, 'so not that long to wait.'

Their conversation stuttered into a silence none of them knew how to fill. Neither Albert nor George had seen much of either of Jessie's children.

'So,' began John, 'shall I tell you the … well, the order of play?'

Borys had begun his usual twitching.

'No need,' said Charles Lyons, joining them. 'Let me tell you. Cars here at ten thirty or so, and then the police will come, and we'll set off for the church at ten to eleven or so. Sneller's cars will be here at the beginning and at the very end, so to speak … So, all you need to do is be ready for quarter to. Once you're there, you'll be directed to your seats by the stewards – Borys, John, you'll be on the right-hand side of the church, at the front, the first pew. Mr George, and ah – Mr George – you'll be behind them. With Mr Curle and – well, after that's settled, we're in Father Sheppard's hands.'

Borys farted loudly.

'Gosh!' he said. 'Sorry, everybody,' and he moved to the other end of the room as Lyons said, 'All done then. Ask me any questions as and when?'

Walter said, 'You can answer that one,' and he and Albert roared.

'We better go up and see Mum and the girls,' Albert suggested and Walter nodded.

John went upstairs to get dressed. He did so slowly, not forgetting to place the pen in his left inside pocket. He tied his tie tight against the top shirt button. It felt like battle. He wanted this to be done, over, finished, to be yesterday. But the day had barely begun.

*

John came back down in black, his white shirt stiff with Audrey's starch. He sat out in the sun, squinting at the yew hedge and shining his brogues like an automaton. He could hear the swish, brush, brush, swish as his hand went to and fro behind the heel, by the side, over the toecap, slowly shining the leather. He spat lightly on the polish and began brushing again. He had begun humming, under his breath, a hymn he had sung at school.

There, suddenly, was Uncle Walter who cheerily observed, 'You were always so easily startled, Jackilo,' and, kindly, his uncle then grinned.

John stopped what he'd been doing and looked at him. Walter George looked like an uncle: his thin, creamy face, slicked-back, ash blond hair, cut that morning, the whiff of a side-street barber's cheap cologne still evident. Walter had hardly any wrinkles, save those that creased round his eyes when he smiled. Walter's brogues were sharp-toed, polished, brilliant above the pinstriped trousers. John could see the shadow of his uncle in the brilliant black. No wing collar, but a thinly knotted black silk tie, leather gloves, silk top hat.

'You gave me a surprise,' said John.

'Well, I came as a ...' and Walter misjudged the moment and growled theatrically, '*GHOST*.'

John stood.

'How was Mama?' Walter said.

'Wet eyed as usual.' John interrupted the silence that followed with, 'I think now is a good time for me to put these shoes on.'

*

Borys was standing in the kitchen, a glass of milk in his hand. He looked out at Bell's farm, and then at the stove. He was still reliving the embarrassment of a few moments earlier. He was petrified of smells, his own smells. He usually squirmed with disgust when Philip's nappy needed changing.

Borys stood at the table, his palms placed straight on the oak. He looked at his mottled hands as if they were not his own, the wrinkling skin on the left knuckles like four eyes. Borys had arrived at that stage in life when one should no longer be surprised at what can be done with flesh.

John walked in with his shoes and put them down by the kitchen door.

'I know I shouldn't count these things,' said Borys with a sniff, 'but that's the forty-ninth telegram.'

'And?' said John. 'Was *he* not worthy of such undying regard?' Borys brushed this comment off.

Perhaps, John thought briefly, he had not registered what he had asked him.

'It's not been like this since you were born.' A forced smile puckered up beneath his too small moustache. 'Suddenly, we're popular again.'

'Were things different when … I don't know – what happened when I was born? You were … you were eight.'

'I was eight. Yes. We were up in London, staying at Uncle Jack's. A lovely summer.' John watched Borys fall back on old times. 'Holland Park … You know – he never played games with us, did he? When Pip comes at me, I stick my thumb in his ear or his mouth, or in *my* mouth, and Joan lets him crawl on me and Pip goes trit-trot, trit-trot on my knee and all I think of is sitting on a 'bus with my father. We'd sit on the 'bus, when you were born, when you were being born, and we'd go to Marble Arch from Shepherd's Bush and back again. Always on the top deck, so I could watch the driver. Papa bought tickets to Marble Arch, on arrival back at Shepherd's Bush, he did it again, the whole journey, four or five times a day. I … I don't remember much about then. 'Buses. Cakes. Mama with her knee, Addison Road.'

'What else do you remember?'

'Your boxing with me.' John took this as a joke, but it seemed not to be as Borys repeated it, in a sober undertone, 'Your boxing.'

'Boxing?' said John.

'You don't know what it's like to have you as a younger brother.' Borys' colour was sapping, his mouth shaking and dribbling as he spoke, his hands raised as though swatting flies from his head or hair, his fingers coming up to his mouth. 'I'd watch – he'd build you paper boats, or play chess, he'd say you were a *diabolito* and giggle with Don Roberto about your being a pagan – and I'd be nothing. You got the Meccano—'

'Uncle André bought that,' John interrupted.

'You've still got it.' Borys had pulled himself together again. 'You got him to get you to climb a tree. To play chess, read … you got him as a father and I, I … I got playing snooker with Hugh.'

Borys took one last gulp from the glass on the kitchen table and said solemnly, 'I was never a boy,' through the ghost of a milk moustache.

John said, 'We're no longer boys, brother,' and heard Borys say, 'Oh, John!' He saw his brother sag before he righted himself, as they heard the cars and Borys muttered something smudged through tears. John heard the gravel.

The hearse had arrived.

The brothers moved outside, leaving the front door ajar as their uncles followed. Scally scrambled after them and, running to the hearse, almost immediately raised one of his back legs against a tyre and then moved off to the back of the vehicle, tongue out, tail wagging.

'We need to get going, Jack,' said Borys, speaking rapidly, the military man, all alert timing and precision. 'Thing starts in forty minutes. I'm going up to Mama, say goodbye and all that. Come with me.'

Someone demanded, 'Could someone just move that bloody dog?'

Audrey came from the porch and attempted to take Scally by his collar.

The policeman remarked that he would happily kick the animal, if that was what was needed.

*

From her bedroom, Jessie heard the closing of car doors. She moved slowly down the corridor, steadying herself with the cane, her left hand up against the wall. She reached the room where he had died, and walked very slowly to the window, where she leant against the sill.

'Mama,' said Borys, opening the door.

'Darling,' she answered, turning slowly towards her child.

'We're off, John and me – and the rest.' She saw John behind him, holding himself by the door. 'We'll be back, as soon as we can be. We'll be back for lunch.'

'Borys,' she said. 'There is no rush, darling. What has to happen has to happen.'

John said, thinking he should smile, 'We'll be thinking of you.'

'Of course you will,' she said. 'I'll be thinking of you,' she replied, looking at him but speaking to his brother.

*

Seen from her husband's bedroom, above the porch, Lyons' back was towards her, and Jessie could not make out what he was saying. Lyons walked back to the house, with Vinten, Foote and the hearse driver and, of all people, Sneller. She could see none of their faces, only their heads, angled from above.

John and Borys were looking into the house. Jessie could see John's left arm behind his back, his hand clenched then fingers flexing like a pianist. Borys stood, she observed with pride, erect, stiff like the soldier he had once been. She was warmed by Borys being there for his brother, her boys together. The feeling dissolved as Lyons gradually walked backwards from the house, his top hat held before him, the coffin coming towards him, borne by Vinten and Foote at the front, the driver and Curle at the back. Jessie thought, oddly, of the owl she had heard the night after his death and how it would see all this, and turned to look back into his bedroom, at the bed – that bed – and the emptiness.

His room. It had hardly been touched since Sunday. The body had been removed. Borys had said it should be left as it was when he was alive, and no one had entered it since his body had been taken down to the study. The bare boards. The books, some of them still splayed open on the bed sheet – a biography of Napoleon, Forster's *A Passage to India*. Three tables, the willow-patterned 'Cigarette Jug', a Spratt's dog-biscuit box. His monocle. Each item seemed to Jessie both filled with him and devoid of anything. She had an image of him in this room, his beard slightly untrimmed, gazing at a map of Elba, a cigarette in his bandaged hand.

That was before the other night – suddenly the last night – when she had been with him here, after she had ordered the new bed for him, and he had looked at it and raged at her. He called it a catafalque. He had accused her of buying him a catafalque and yelled at her, stomping up and down the hall, his hands windmilling, and he had gone to his room without kissing her, for the only time in their married life.

He had gone to this bed without kissing her.

When she next looked out of the window, the coffin was in the hearse. Doors were clunking shut again, the cars' engines turned on. Jessie pressed her head against the cool pane of the window. On the sill was a packet of cigarettes. Jessie snatched it up, rattled it by her ear, and quickly pocketed the box in her dressing gown.

*

The junior policeman leant himself forward, taking off his hat.

'I thought we might take Frog Lane, then turn off to go past the house, and then on, through the village, through Bridge, on the Dover Road past the cricket club and then on, take the right onto Bridge Street and left into Burgate, stopping just after in front of the church.' Curle nodded and looked up at

Charles Lyons. 'Shouldn't take us twenty minutes, despite the cricket.'

Lyons smiled in agreement. 'I'll go on ahead,' he said, meaning he would be driven in the hearse. Lyons and the policeman had a few words before the policeman straddled his bicycle and started off, wobbling a bit as he looked back to see if the procession had begun to follow him, which it had not.

*

Jessie stumbled from his bedroom and with her hands against the walls walked slowly down the corridor to her own, where her mother was fussing with the pillows on her bed and her sister Florence tucking in the bedspread.

'Audrey can do that later,' Jessie said.

'I told her to go and prepare the sandwich spread,' said her mother. Noticing the cortège from Jessie's window, Jane George croaked to her daughters, 'Watch them for as long as you can,' and Florence helped Jessie stand as the cars drove off up the hill, swallows darting in the sky.

Jessie took one look and saw the cars behind the hearse and the sight of their sons, again her children, and turned away. She had lived through some of what followed – the death of a father – and pitied them, for they had not.

*

The journey surprised John, mostly because it was spent in silence, interrupted only by inanity, and the car backfiring, taking so long, yet also over so soon. He had imagined this would be the time when Borys might actually say something to him worth saying. John realized that again he had been optimistic.

For the first time in a long time, John looked out of the window and noticed instead what lay on the route. What they had come to know as Borys' tree, then the pond by Bourne House, and then the drive into Bridge, past the butcher, open now but the staff lined up outside and looking at the cortège or at their shoes, as were the staff from The White Horse, where John had watched his father drink whisky and soda, watching him as he watched others. '*Quis custodiet ipsos custodes?*' his father would mutter as they played chess, always before enabling his bishop for an un-ecclesiastical moment of slaughter. 'The bishop is out for blood, not tea,' John had quoted smartly during their last game, removing his father's queen from the board. JC had laughed.

On the Dover Road, the ugly yellow brick cottages, tea cloths and blue sheets, an apron on a drying line, life going on. John noticed once more the slowness of the car, watching the hearse before them almost crawling towards the city, realizing Borys had still said nothing. What *was* going on in his head? John looked at his brother, and watched him for a while: drumming his fingers on the black silk of his top hat, and then fiddling with his cufflinks, pushing down the white shirt cuffs so as to be even all round the black of his jacket sleeve, his fingers tidying the knot of his tie. And then, something John had somehow known would happen though he had not seen it for years, something his brother had not done since they were boys: Borys raised his fingers to his lips, licked them, and dried them on the knee of his trousers.

The hearse was drawing into Canterbury, its passage slowed by the other traffic. They had crossed St Lawrence's and Ethelbert Road, where their mother's most recent operation had taken place, where she had stayed while their father had failed at home. John tried to read the number plate of the car before them, thinking he should remember this, hold this thing above all else, this detail, something to recall. He turned to look at his brother again. Borys was staring through the other side window, at the pub, at the terraced houses. On his side, the left side, John now had a long blank wall, geraniums, men and boys walking the other way to watch the cricket match.

Neither seemed to have a thing to say to one another now their father was dead, and John realized that this journey marked a line beyond which they would never really speak to one another as brothers again, merely as men who had once had the same father.

'Jackilo,' Borys began, and John was surprised into a 'Yes.'

He stopped glancing at the view, and gazed at Borys who said, 'I don't … you know, they have a collection at these things, don't they?'

John let the silence between them lie.

'Did you remember to bring some change?'

John wriggled his fingers in his pockets and both heard the dulled sound of coins.

'Yes,' he said, 'I've got something.'

John's lower jaw was rigid and his hand had reached for his wallet as his brother said, 'I wondered if I might—' and John presented a pound note. Then he looked at his brother, and made his brother look at him and John understood immediately what people would say for some time to come: that he was old before his years.

John said, 'You *are* the elder. Be *seen* to be.'

Borys took the money, sheepishly slipping John's folded note into the breast pocket of his mourning coat. John looked at his wristwatch: five past eleven. He glanced at the window, knowing his father might have been proud, at that moment, and then to Borys, glimpsing the dots of blood on the rim of the hard wings of his brother's collar where he had cut himself.

When he was a father, John thought with dimmed anger – when he was buried in half a century or so – his sons would shave the night before, or bring their own money to church or, just, be better.

*

At Oswalds, Jessie sat in the broken armchair by the curved window in her room, listening to the slow tick of the clock on the mantelpiece. She had told her mother and sister she wanted to be alone for the time the service lasted, to be there with *all* her boys. Jessie stared out at the poplars, the rising field towards the road to Canterbury, heard the sparrows hopping on the roof. She had her sons in her mind as they were driven away from her, her boys watching their father's progress into the earth. She saw the light in her room showed moted sunbeams falling towards the green carpet. *He will not come back with them,* she thought. *I am aweary, aweary, O God that I were dead!*

Jessie was aware she was lividly frozen in the chair; the only parts of her body that seemed to move were her eyes and fingers. She came upon the cardboard packet she had found on the window sill in his room. She opened it. One cigarette left. She looked at it. She had never smoked. She had known the smell of a married man, the whiff of whisky, the scent of tobacco, the sour odour of both. Her husband rarely brushed his teeth. When he kissed her, he had a rotten taste: the kiss lasted, not always in a pleasant fashion. She rolled this, his last cigarette in her stubby fingers and put its tip to her lips and she sucked it in, unlit. Her cheeks were, immediately, lined with tears. She breathed in deeply and then removed the cigarette, small flakes of leaf specking her lips. She spat them out babyishly, making the most polite raspberry. *He will not come back.*

There had been nights when she had sat there, watching a thin slice of the moon in the sky and hearing him laugh, or type, or pace around in the study below. Now she sat in a silence smoothly interrupted by the phutting of a far passing car, by the footsteps of her family below.

She had asked her mother and sister to go downstairs and leave her for a moment, while she collected herself. She had told them a lie. What she wanted to do was to open the cigarette packet and smoke with him in silence.

There was a cough at the door. Jessie put her cigarette hurriedly back into its box, in doing so broke the thing, and hid the empty packet beneath the cushion behind her.

She said, 'Come in!' and saw Florence looking anxious, embarrassed and useless. 'Oh, Flo,' and then, 'To think, we were married in the same church, you and Sarge, me and him,' and both of them halted, took this fact in and then sobbed and sobbed and sobbed until Audrey arrived, to be sure nobody else had died.

*

As the hearse arrived in Burgate, John heard, then felt the vibrations from the muffled toll of the bell of St Thomas the Martyr.

Before the motor had stopped, doors opened. Charles Lyons was standing, his hand on the door handle. John stepped out onto the cobbles. His brother peered over the bonnet and looked over at the next car drawing up. For one moment John wondered if Borys was actually going to ask to look at the engine.

A few other men in black were at the church door. Lyons closed the door of the car with the same smoothness with which he had opened it, and brought out the wreath that had been lying on the coffin. Father Sheppard moved from the others by the porch and took John's hand, then held Borys' hand as well and talked to him, the elder. John realized a strange, sudden feeling of not really being present. *Am I here, now, at my father's funeral? Am I now here? Is this happening?*

'We should go in,' said Sheppard. 'Or rather,' a priestly grin, 'you should.' Borys smiled back and put his hat back on.

'Take it off,' John commanded in a whisper. He looked to Uncle Albert. 'Uncle Albert,' he began, calmly, 'Borys and I have … can we … I spoke with Uncle Dick earlier, so, could you …?' and Albert nodded, stepping forward. John noticed again the points of his extraordinarily sharp shoes, his leather gloves, the silk hat.

Father Sheppard turned to John, who then said

something his father may have said, 'Have you served the parish long?' and John felt so adult saying so, saying the right thing – the charmingly, appropriately null thing to say. This was the moment when John realized people – even priests – say things to say things simply, not to *mean* things.

Father Sheppard hurried on with his answer, 'Twenty-one years this year. And I've never buried an author. But then, Father Anthony will be taking the service – you *do* remember him?'

All John could stutter was, 'Not now,' and he was suddenly inside the church.

The place smelled – a word that ricocheted in his head: *smelled*. What do churches smell *of*? Cold stone, damp, hot candle wax, the cold air by draughty windows, old men's shoes, damp hassocks and new Guerlain, polished pews and the pages of a new prayer book.

John looked around him – Garnett was there, and he saw Ralph Wedgwood. A dozen or more familiar faces, seriously stricken with sadness. They walked towards the high altar, the white marble lit by the sun streaming through the stained glass.

Curle was at the end of a pew. John and Borys were shown to the pew by the font.

The service began. For John it took no time at all,

the flower-smothered coffin brought in, meaning less than ever. The coffin was covered in purple cloth, lying on the true catafalque. John listened to the Latin and heard all, though understood little. In the days that passed, this had taken five minutes, or so it seemed to him.

Father Milton said, '*Ite missa est*,' and his hand rose to bless them all.

They responded, '*Deo gratias*,' and then, very deliberately, the congregation rose with the first three, slow, staccato chords from the organ. The Death March.

Borys was already on his feet before John knew he had to stand. He looked across the aisle to Curle, who nodded to him very gently, encouraging him. John was struck to see Don Roberto standing by him – where had *he* come from? He looked thinner, still dapper, his eyes swivelling round the church, taking everything in. His face looked as if it had recently been through a pencil sharpener. Breakfast's jam and toast still lodged in his lower beard. Or was it dried blood?

The chords were repeated now, higher and louder, as Borys turned to his brother and they both moved out into the middle of the aisle. John made out more faces – Dr Tebb, and Canon Ashton-Gwatkin, the fellow from the stationers on the High Street, Goulden's, and Mrs Rothenstein and the dignitaries from London Curle had said would be there, and John finally saw the face he knew he had been looking for: Miss Hallowes. Elegant in black, with nothing more than herself there, absorbed in reading the order of service.

Borys and he walked out and, as they did, John watched the juddering shadow of the organist on the stone floor as he played and, turning his head up to the window, the four solemn faces of the choir looking down.

Among all these people, he felt disastrously alone. John abruptly wanted his mother to be there, to go out into the city with them all. For a moment he imagined himself outside, behind her wheelchair, it bumping over the cobbles behind the coffin, her hard shoulders pinched with pain.

At the back of the church, just to the left of the door, were Vinten and Foote, which did not seem right: Foote, the man first in the room when his father had died, his head bowed as John screwed up his eyes against the glare of the sunlight outside, the organ wheezing boisterously now.

John stood by his brother and watched as the door of the hearse was shut. Burgate was quiet, and the people who happened to be there stood in silence. John watched a boy younger than he was, holding a tray outside the butchers. As John looked more closely, faces turned to the pavement, and all John could see were people's heads looking down, one woman crossing herself before doing so.

When the hearse had started up, the party started walking. John walked, his eyes on the car then above it, drawn by the sun glinting in the copper of the new memorial. John noticed Borys look at it and turn sharply away, towards the Cathedral. There, at Christ Church Gate, cricketers saluted, and John imagined what his father might feel if he were alive inside the car, not dead in a box, what he might think inside the coffin, the skin of some wild beast inside. Where was that beast now? The men lined up at the shop windows, by the hotel and the town hall, the banks, the pubs and the tea shops, by Goulden's shop, all decked in white for sport, or violet and crimson, in pinks and blues and shades of green.

John was there in the world, and the world was continuing, the whole parade was going on: but he was not part of it – none of them were *part* of it. They all remained inept, in a bubble of respect.

*

Leaving the church, Lilian Hallowes told Charles Lyons she would walk, and remembered, '*Steer north,*' *he said.*

Sitting four rows back, on the left side, Lilian had seen Ralph Wedgwood, and Edward Garnett, but she was surprised to see the Dean there, and by how small the congregation was. She had hoped John would not notice but now, in the open air, it seemed as if both of the boys might. The coffin appeared, undraped, in the dazzling sun and Lilian moved away, her back against the flinty wall. Cunninghame Graham was there, finally.

Men followed the coffin, and Lilian held back until Cunninghame Graham saw her. He beamed. They had met before, perhaps twice.

'*Vamos,*' he said, almost intimately, his hand on her shoulders. 'I was getting sick of that Roman stuff.'

'There's more to come,' she stated with no thought, but it made them both laugh.

Cunninghame Graham said to her, 'It's very good to see you again. He told me *all about you,*' at which point Lilian finally started to cry. Their pace slowed.

Cunningham Graham took her hand, then held it firmly as she placed herself back into decency.

*

The walk from St Thomas' to the cemetery took fifteen minutes.

John was conscious of walking through a city and yet there were reminders that that city was small as a town, stalled for him between words and worlds. Beside the cortège as it moved in a horse-trot onto the High Street and up the hill, men stood tending haycocks, boy scouts lolled in breeches, farmers dozed in dogcarts, men in whites stood, their faces bowed holding the hands of their girls tightly, every face with its meaning slightly rubbed off it now. John saw some bullocks being driven by a man in a cart marked 'ABATTOIR'. He looked back at the West Gate and then his head turned to watch the hearse as it drove up the hill.

The cortège stopped at the cemetery gates. John looked over the small throng of men, some women, all dressed in black. There were faces he knew, faces he had seen at the church for the service, but there were also new faces, people who had come for the interment, people he recognized. Faces of friends of his parents, people he had known as a child though now he could not recall their names, only remembering their features or faded hairlines, their well-meaning smiles, the style of their clothing or their mannerisms. John was struck by a well of friendship he could not make any sense of, people who had come here, now, out of love, or mere curiosity. Men would look at him and see him as a boy and so would their wives and they would smile at his adulthood and it pained him, this continued loss of innocence.

Lyons nodded to Borys and Borys said, 'We're going this way.'

John followed them in silence to the space in the ground where the coffin would be laid. Into his mind came the same words from the morning: *I am going to see my father buried. I am come to bury my father.* And somehow, atrociously, from a play they had performed two years earlier at school, the words *Not Caesar.*

*

Swathes of purple felt were spread welcomingly either side of the damp brown hole, flowers already sapped by the sun, a clod of soil for the priest to crumble onto the coffin.

The sons walked up towards the hole and then,

with their uncles, stepped back. John was briefly shocked by the seeming finality of that space, unable to take his eyes from the freshly dug earth.

Charles Lyons walked over to Father Sheppard and handed him a few sheets of paper and a book.

Sheppard cleared his throat dramatically.

There is no echo in the open air, John thought, *just emptiness, the emptiness of air.* Where is a voice without its echo? *Hear, O Lord, my prayer ...*

Father Sheppard stood in silence. His body became something, his face the thing to watch. The crucifer stood, the cross wobbling uncertainly in his adolescent arms. John observed two boys he thought he knew from junior school, standing with the cross, candles unlit. Sheppard grinned at him widely, like Maskelyne – the toothy grin struck him, his eyes theatrically opened and widened, and John realized he had never understood these words until he saw what he then saw: Sheppard's eyes *opened.*

'My friends, my friends, we have some other business.'

No hesitation, supposed John. *Get him under ground.*

The priest's hands rose, his fingers seemed to grow in the air and Sheppard spoke again, '*Praeceptis salutaris moniti, et divina institutione formati, audemus dicere.'*

John thought of that hand in the air, reminded of something he had seen in Paris once, painted by El Greco, Sheppard's fingers quivering meaning into nothing and commanding everyone to say something. The Paternoster began, ending with, *'sed libera nos a malo,'* spoken by all including, to his surprise, John.

Once again the words came at him. *Libera nos a malo*. Sheppard stood, not like any other priest from any other church:

> *De profundis clamavi ad te, Domine:*
> *Domine, exaudi vocem meam:*
> *Fiant aures tuae intendentes,*
> *in vocem deprecationis meae.*
> *Si iniquitates observaveris, Domine:*
> *Domine, quis sustinebit?*

Sheppard looked around and stared at Borys, then at John. He whispered, 'Lord, who shall stand it?' and the greying whites of both his eyes bulged at them, although perhaps only John saw this, and only John heard the screech of seagulls high above. Sheppard had begun to move around the hole, his hands to the heavens,

'Deus, cujus miseratione animæ fidelium requiescunt, hunc tumulum benedicere dignare, eique angelum tuum sanctum deputa custodem: et quorum quarumque corpora hic sepeliuntur, animas eorum ab omnibus absolve vinculis delictorum; ut in te semper cum Sanctis tuis sine fine lætentur. Per Christum Dominum nostrum.'

Another 'Amen', stronger this time, sounded into the sky. One of the boys with his holy face moved to Sheppard and he took the aspergillum, silently mouthing words that John knew and did not believe – *Adveniat regnum tuum* and another *sed libera nos a malo* – and Sheppard shook it over the grave, over the coffin, and handed the rod to John.

John had seen this before, but he had done it infrequently: he had watched what other boys had done. So he took the thing and, when he sensed he should, gave it back quickly, his face sprinkled with the stuff.

It seemed alien. All John wanted was to talk with his father, just once more, and for him to say something back.

As in the church, words were spoken and John heard them, not taking them in until he watched the handful of soil being thrown onto the dropped coffin.

Father Sheppard stopped his Latin prayers and broke into English. A man John had never set eyes on before, carrying by far and away the largest floral tribute he had seen, was now nodding to Father Sheppard.

The fellow next to him was translating from Polish and said to Sheppard, 'He's asking if it's his … go – I mean, turn. Actually, if it's time for him to …'

Sheppard's head bent in agreement and prayer. 'It is.'

And the Pole said in a voice loud enough, 'These are words I wish to say now here, which one day meant a great deal to Korzeniowski, and to us all who will miss him, and they are:

Chrystus niech mi bedzie grodem,
Krzyż niech bedzie mym przewodem,
łaska pokrop, życie daj!

Kiedy ciało me się skruszy,
Oczyszczonej w ogniu duszy
Glorje zgotuj niebo, raj.'

Sheppard motioned to Borys and John to come forward, and Borys seemed to know what to do. He pulled a lily from the wreath and threw it into the hole and John did the same. Sheppard was saying

'Amen' and it would be, John saw, very nearly time for everyone to leave.

*

Lilian noticed George Bell. He was wearing a black cloak, a red soutane, white ribbons from his dog collar. This time he looked trim, rosy-cheeked, almost holidayed, his sandy hair newly cut. Lilian knew she had taken against the Dean for some reason and then she saw why: he looked as if he were *enjoying* himself.

'I didn't expect to see you so soon,' she said to him, calmly.

'I didn't either. I didn't know you were *his* secretary.' That sleek voice again, so different from his public one.

'You didn't get much of a chance to ask.'

They paused, truly examining one another for the first time.

'I saw you leave the Eucharist early and then, the following day, then I worked out why.'

Lilian looked at him, her mind moving towards memory.

Bell took his grey-blue glance away and spotted a gravedigger by the wall. He knew his name. *Smith?*

No – he couldn't be called Smith. Bell turned to Miss Hallowes.

'Are you going with the family to the pub?'

Lilian looked at him, sharply. 'Which one?'

'The Unicorn.'

'No.'

'Well, would you join me for tea at the Deanery?'

'No,' she said again, and wished John were with her now so she could smoke a cigarette with him somewhere secret. 'Not really my sort of thing, not now,' Lilian admitted. 'I'm not very good with death.'

Bell came to her, and took her hand.

'Don't.'

He dropped her hand and made to touch her elbow, to hold her somehow.

'Don't touch me.'

Bell said he was sorry. He began, 'The loss of a good friend—'

Lilian stopped him and said, 'Do you know what I *hate* about your God?' her outstretched hand up, almost in his face. 'You've *worked out why*. Well – it's that. It allows *you*,' her forefinger was stabbing in the air at him now, 'It allows you all *that*. But you're wrong. You were wrong. I didn't leave because he was dead. The loss of a good friend, the soul will go to heaven, the tears will be mopped up by angels, the game will go on – go on and on. There's never checkmate with the Church, is there. Is there?'

Bell took a deep breath.

Lilian said, 'Not the place for that, not here, not now.' She clenched her fists, then adjusted her hat and checked her hair with the palm of her hand and said more easily, lightly and with much less sincerity, 'Perhaps another time?'

And then Lilian walked away.

*

'We should wait here,' ordered Borys. 'Lyons said we should thank people for coming. So: let's wait here, till we're told what to do next.'

One of the men from the *Kent Herald* Lyons had allowed to be there was taking a list.

John said, 'I don't know who half of them are, do you?'

His brother was suffering in the heat.

'Borys?' offered John. He nearly tried to touch his brother.

'Do you think I can have a cigarette now?' asked Borys.

John replied softly, 'No.' He watched Borys' thumb stumbling on the flint of a lighter repeatedly, on his father's – his dead father's – lighter. John said, 'I think *he* would have approved. He'd probably have gasped through a packet and a half by now. No? But I think Mama would be horrified. *She'd* hate it.'

Borys flicked the flint once and put the lighter back into his waistcoat pocket.

'So,' said John, 'who *are* these people?'

Borys was looking at the shine on his shoes.

John appealed, 'Help me.'

He needed to see Lilian.

*

John knew what he had to do. As they passed he grasped each man's hand and listened to whatever he had to say. Borys, in front of him, did the same, only with more speed.

It felt to John as though he was not really there, not here in a cemetery, now, but on they came, as he remembered his father had once told him, the good, the bad, the sad and the cheerful, the younger ones following, a column of consolation. Here was the man younger than Curle from Poland, Count Raczyński.

Only when, having asked a question in his

infantile second tongue, the ambassador announced, 'From London,' did John think he might do this in a different way, even though the ambassador looked into John's eyes and said, '*Ojciec jest tutaj.*'

So he shook the man's hand, smiling as he said, 'Thank you for coming.'

There were some faces he knew: Fred from the Fleur-de-Lys, who had bought John a drink once and bored his father about how much a master mariner's ration of gin was; and the stationer from the High Street, where they had gone to pick up writing paper; an odd fellow from Latin America wearing too many black clothes – bizarrely, wearing a white tie and a black shirt – identified later as Altamirano, who according to Cunninghame Graham should not have been there at all, he was just someone who had bumped into their father by accident twenty or so years before, but John thought it strangely touching he had bothered to turn up at all; and an unfamiliar Methodist, Zelie, with his American accent which unsettled John, and reminded him of what Borys had once told him about 'Yankee chaplains'.

And on they came until Borys said, 'We must go and look at the wreaths now. Charley says so.'

*

Lilian had walked away from Bell in a trance of shy rage, unaware precisely where she was walking. She was observing a doomed rose bush, the flowers crinkling in the summer sun, when she found herself kicking the torso of a workman dozing in the sun, his back against the chapel wall: she had knocked a man over.

When he came to, his legs and arms hauling himself upright, he was spluttering and mumbling, but politely. His smock was muddied, the wrinkles on his face and forehead caked in earth, brown stains – not from the soil – on his teeth.

Lilian apologized, said she had not seen him there.

He said nothing and struck a match instead.

'Quite a busy time of year,' he said after a while, as if explaining why he was tired. 'The heat – gets to the old folk in August. Cricket week, always busy for us. Not that *he* was that old,' and he nodded towards the grave, now delicately bringing the tip of his cigarette into glowing life.

Something in Lilian also flickered. 'Did *you* know Mr Conrad?'

'Of course.' The man said nothing more: he had delivered a fact.

'I *worked* with him.'

'Well, I didn't,' and the chap grinned brownly. 'He would come down here. He'd walk around the graves, have a few words with us – we'd go off towards the West Gate, and he'd treat me and Albert to a gin.'

'You *knew* him.' Lilian was taken aback. Here was the afternoon's first surprise. She said nothing until this formed in her head, 'Is it *odd* to dig the grave of a man you *know*?' and suddenly the question was out.

The man blinked at her. 'It's a hole. I'm sorry. It's a hole. It's always just another hole to me. What's *odd* is what goes into it.'

'Miss Hallowes?'

Lilian turned away from the gravedigger. John's much missed voice was calling to her. She had been unaware that the procession had been coming back. She saw that Jessie's brothers and a cluster of other familiar faces were behind John, the uncles shepherding Borys away, everyone tired and trying to reach their cars, and John drifting away from them all.

'John,' she said, watching the gravedigger doddering off towards the cemetery gates.

'It is so good to see you, so good of you …' He stopped himself repeating what all the others had said to him. 'I am going to have to go home, they want me to go off for something, and then home, and Mama, and our grandmother is with us and – well, it's time for me, for us to go.'

Not for the first time, Lilian noticed the impossibility of chat, the softness of communication. She felt apart from it. *Friends again, yet aware they would meet no more,* as she had read the night before.

John asked her, 'What will you be doing?' and Lilian found herself admitting, 'I shall go down to Wimborne, to see George and Lil, to stay a few weeks with them. I'll need to find new work at their … but …' and she stood rigid, the order of service sticking out from her handbag, a bead or two of tear spilt upon her cheek.

'Can I do anything?' he asked in a near whisper.

Lilian shook her head. 'I might ask Eric or your mother to borrow that typewriter,' she said.

John moved further away from the family, from Cunninghame Graham deep in conversation with the ambassador, towards her. John looked around him, not wanting to be seen, his right hand reaching in his coat for something, shifting his gaze here and there before looking intently into her own grey eyes.

'You know, Miss H., that … I hope we'll talk again, in time. Now, I must go. But whatever you do, *ask for the typewriter*. Remember this: please – *ask for the typewriter.*'

John then conjured from his palm a handkerchief, white silk, which he pressed into her hand.

'You won't get it. Borys and Mama won't let you, I know that.'

His hand was hard.

'Take this,' he said, glimpsing his sudden glare of snow. 'Goodbye Miss Hallowes,' he said, quietly, as he stepped back into the throng.

Lilian put the handkerchief and whatever else he had put inside it into her coat pocket. She did not need to dry her eyes now.

John said formally and slightly too loudly, 'Thank you for being here with us. We, we all thank you.'

He moved, she thought, to kiss her then brought out his hand again to shake hers instead. To her, he was – rather too suddenly – no longer that little boy.

'It was very good, so good, of you to come,' he was saying.

And then Lilian thought John did something peculiar. *Did he?* Lilian would think later that evening.

John could never have winked at his father's funeral. But she knew he had.

So did John.

*

People began dispersing. Lilian did not know what to do, where to go, when to go. She had not been told what the family had planned, but now it appeared there was to be a gathering at The Unicorn. If Mrs C. had been with them, plans would have been different. Lilian looked at her wristwatch and planned an escape, so as not to be the last.

She moved over to the grave and then knelt, slowly, silently sighing to herself. *Steer north*, words he had written for her, and she pondered his voice and being there for him and his kindnesses, the smile, the upward gaze as he laughed, his finger jabbing at birds on the lawn, giving a finch its name, and then she moved away. She was aware she was empty.

Her walk took her south.

Jean-Aubry came up and took her by the arm saying that he would be in touch, and Lilian knew that he would not, that *he* was off without her and then she nodded to Don Roberto who came up to her and said, 'How lovely of us all to be here to

remember him. *Stabat pater doloroso*, at the end, eh?'
and then he was carried away by more men, chatting
as they walked to the cemetery entrance.

She was intent on leaving, past the graves of the
Salvatores and the Megliococcas and onto the road
where she knew she could walk downhill towards St
Dunstan's and the station. The wrong station, but
somewhere to take her away from here.

John had demanded, with strange insistency, *Ask
for the typewriter.*

Lilian walked down the hill alone. For much of
her life she had been *called* a typewriter, and now her
profession was the name of a sort of machine. She
had to steady herself every now and then, losing her
balance, passing the pub where she realized Conrad
and the men who had dug his grave must have drunk
their gin, and then she stopped, dazzled by the glare
of the sun from the glass of passing cars. The George
brothers, Don Roberto waving at some cricketers,
another car, Borys' head, John must have been in the
same vehicle which indeed he was, looking out at the
other side from Lilian, out at the crowds and their
lives, life going on. In the car, John was amazed by the
hush, the stillness despite the noise.

As the car vanished past Lilian, turning the
corner after the church, Lilian's view was an imagined

version of John's – all the world covered in snow: an icy silence.

*

They had forty-five minutes at The Unicorn before the landlord called time. Lyons had arranged for drinks at the back bar, away from the few cricket spectators, and pistachios, sandwiches and apples. A few would carry on to Oswalds for tea.

Curle was asked almost immediately, 'Who was that chap speaking Polish at the end? I couldn't hear Sheppard telling us.' And before he could respond: 'No idea – someone from the embassy, I think. No idea what he was going on about either. But sometimes it's easier just to shut up and let them talk in their own lingo and we all smile along and they feel so much happier about everything, don't they? And then they shut up …'

Then he moved to Garnett and one of Jessie's brothers.

'But we need the money.'

'We all need money. We just shouldn't,' said Garnett, and he raised a salmon sandwich to his mouth. 'We shouldn't talk about it now,' and he popped it in, in one go.

'I have to help Jessie finish John's education,' said Albert, his mouth also full.

'No,' Garnett said sharply, as if he were commanding a dog: '*No!*'

'I have to help them plan for a new home, where *are* they going to … to live? And Borys. I have to help him provide for the baby—'

Garnett's palm was up, as he swallowed some wine. '*You* don't. Borys has a job.' Albert looked frozen at this thought. Garnett continued. 'Stop this now, please,' he was whispering his plea now. 'Now is not the moment.'

'Where are they going to *live?*'

Curle decided enough was enough, and found John, looking lost with half a pint.

'We can go soon,' he said and John smiled.

'Oh good,' he said. 'Thank you, Dick.'

*

Once home, after tea, John went upstairs and observed them all depart. Audrey had made strawberry and cream tartlets and spicy tomato juice for the folk who didn't want tea. Charley told him later that evening she did not really know what she was doing. Joan had packed their luggage in the Daimler so Borys could take them back to King's Cross by five o'clock. Curle had his case in the porch by the door and Sneller was taking him and Cunninghame Graham back to London, where Don Roberto had arranged to stay near Russell Square. Jessie's mother and Nell were staying, but Flo and Sarge were off. The house was, John realized, staffed with servants with not much to do.

He turned to his bed. Two strange, shrivelled, flattened flowers, once white now brown and brittle, lay on the eiderdown. Who had put them there?

They made him want to sneeze, but he had no handkerchief.

At the open window he looked out and slowly heard the world, the crash of the sea in the leaves of the trees around him, water roaring above the earth. His father's home and, now, his.

The house was quiet. It was suddenly as if nothing had happened at all and he was in the middle of another boring summer holiday. In his bedroom John sat on his chair and looked at the kid's things beside him and felt the tears arrive once more.

*

When Lilian returned home she had no luggage. The thought halted her as she took the steps up to the front door of the house where she lived. Something else that was not there – the case that should be tugging at her arm.

As the key slid into the lock, the leaf-brown valise she had had the weekend before, lay inside uncharacteristically unpacked. The wash bag removed, one pair of shoes. The rest would be still there in the case, its lid up, by the wall at the foot of her bed.

She closed the door behind her gently, and smelled the smell that was home, the place where she was. She walked into the kitchen and took off the black coat, and then, leaning against the table, slipped off her shoes.

She half-filled the kettle and settled it on the hob, then lit the gas, before returning to stop the drip-drip of the tap. She took a cup from the draining board and then stopped herself. *Her bedroom.* She put the cup down. She was becoming startled by the happenings of that day. She opened the door.

The case lay there. Lilian did not move. She stood and examined its contents: her folded dress, gloves, a velvet bag with some costume jewellery, the ink, paper, pencils, ribbons and carbon paper, Warren's Bible tucked in one of the three side pockets – and then the notebook. She hoped it might flutter into life. All those words, their time, all that business, all their *life*.

Lilian Hallowes stood and looked and warily picked up the notebook to take it to its usual place on the desk by her bed. She moved then to her chair, where she sat for a long while, her left hand on her chin, one finger covering her lips. Her vision was blurred: she blinked it – the last week – back into focus.

She remembered she had forgotten to buy a present for John. She had meant to have bought him the cufflinks, and she recalled the streets and the Dean and then her failed dash and then her shock and then she knew: above all, she knew she was still in it, still. The shock.

Only then did she remember John's handkerchief.

Lilian unclasped her bag and reached into it, and it was not there. Her coat.

What John had pressed into her hand earlier was not, in fact, his handkerchief. What Lilian retrieved from the ghostly pockets of her unoccupied coat turned out to be a scarf: a creamily silk scarf with black tassels. Within its folds, hidden within the impossible centre of something like a rose, was rolled a fountain pen. When later unscrewed, its carriage half-empty, its nib mottled with ink, the pen was cold, sleek, gold, stolen, given. His and, now, hers.

Lilian looked at it, what remained. She walked

back into the kitchen and placed the pen on the table, and watched it. She picked it up, her fingers stroking its sleek grooves, and suddenly, ruinously, she felt that she had nothing else in this world. This was the pen that had written the cheques for her typing, that had signed her letters, that had inscribed her books, underscored proofs, it had written and over-written and corrected and, often, simply performed a signature, a *JC*, or *J.C.*

She raised the pen to her face and breathed in the nib's odour left to right, under her nose, seeking the old smell of his tobacco or else some other scent of the man, tracing the ink. There was nothing.

Lilian looked at the clock. Nine thirty. Bed.

She looked for something to write on, and found one of her Smythson cards, a present from George two Christmases ago. She wrote,

Dear John,

It was very good to see you and Borys at the funeral and you must pass my wishes to your mother. It was such a difficult day for you all. I shall be writing to her separately.

I shall be down in Dorset soon, but I shall be thinking of you.

Will you let Mr Curle, and Mr Pinker know I

shall be in touch with them soon? If I can help in any way over *Suspense*, or anything else, I shall be only too happy so to do.

Yours sincerely,

Lilian M. Hallowes

She put the card in its envelope, took her pen; it hovered before writing the address, and then did not do so. She would rather no one else knew she had his pen. Lilian brought out her own Sheaffer and scribbled the address.

Where her lips had licked shut the envelope she had girlishly written on one side,

T and on the other Y

knowing nobody else would know.

*

Once in her room, her teeth brushed and her warm face washed in cold, cold water, Lilian sat on her bed and slipped one shoe from her right foot with her left ankle, one from her left with the right. With JC she sometimes wore trousers. A dim din in her head repeated the fact: *There was no JC*. Lilian turned to her shoes. She wanted them placed under her bed:

she loathed the sight of lonely, discarded shoes and did not want her own to be so.

And so it came to be that Lilian was muddled by memory, cluttered by clothes. She stood up, shivering slightly. She removed the black shawl that her other brother had given her for Warren's funeral, draping it on the suitcase by the wall, and then she carefully unbuttoned her blouse, made her skirt slip slowly down to the floor; Lilian sat down again on the edge of her bed to unclip her stockings, sliding them from her legs with an almost knowing ease. She stood and, closing her eyes, slipped off her undergarments. When she raised her arms behind her and felt the known, silent beats of each naked breast on her chest, she knew again something of herself, her shoulders and the nape of her neck in the mirror, the shock of the darkness round her nipples but – not now – no, she would not look at herself now.

Her hair was long, but from the age of thirteen its length had never been seen by others. In public it was always pinned up, and there came the moment every night when she removed the bobby pin and she felt the sensation on her shoulders, caressing her back. She would lie in bed and twist its strands in her hands, amazed that this stuff belonged to her, that it was her.

For the first time in a long time, she slid herself between the crisp linen sheets wearing nothing. *Naked came I out of my mother's womb, and naked shall I return thither.* She felt her worn body between those sheets, her feet searching out the corners of the white, cold, starched linen.

What was new again was the feel of hair against her skin and the manner in which she was excited by her own nakedness. Lilian deliberated, surprising herself, what it might be like to lie with someone again, feeling another's tongue inside her once more, and perhaps with him, when he had been alive or with John, or with a kind man like Curle, or with Dora, reliably unreliable, who she had met and liked – *'We have too much in common … Have you never been in love?'* – and never properly known. It was all impossible.

Lilian rose and stood, naked. She had not drawn the curtains and she looked down now, below, at the garden. Immediately she was watching a fox outside, gazing at the animal, its brush quivering, and as suddenly Lilian closed the drapes, she understood she was not made for sex: she was made for work and she returned to her bed. She reached for the light to click its switch and turn the darkness on. She felt her own heat against the sheets – *but how can one be warm alone?* – and she closed her eyes and held her eyelids tight to seek more darkness, a game she had played since she had been a little girl, one she had refined after Warren's death. She had almost told John that her brother had shot himself that day nineteen years ago, yet there was no point in him knowing such violence now; she almost sought to wrap herself into that darkness and tried to see nothing – no light, no sound, now, no thing – nothing, until there was *nothing in this world*, nothing, *nothing more in the world to write about, nothing. There is nothing in this world but other people, nothing to be afraid of*, her ghost would read. *Nothing*. Lilian dwelt for a while on this – words JC had written, dictated, said to her again and again: nothing in this world.

Her head, her legs and toes and elbows and calves, the fingers that cracked when she flexed them every morning, the knotty strands of her hair grazing her bending neck, her whole body gradually found more warmth and form on her pillow, above the lumpy mattress, rippling the blankets as the sharp linen cold of her sheets lessened.

In Lilian's mind feelings and memories echoed, resonated, like the incisive treble voice she had heard in the Cathedral nave days before. *I am almost a thief. Absence so much more present than presence. I'm ready when you are. Is it* odd *to dig the grave of a man you know? Ask for the typewriter. That glimpse of truth for which you have forgotten to ask.*

Her pillowcase was already damp.

Before she drifted to sleep that Thursday night, her mind filling and emptying and attempting to avoid her thoughts, Lilian realized that the dead are with us because we live so quickly and die so slowly: as we sleep, something of us departs – we fall towards slumber, slope towards the end. When she was gone those who would never know him or her would still hear their voices: we will live with them today, whenever today will be.

Lilian breathed fitfully at first, panicked by such notions then, calmly, unknowingly she slowed her musings and imaginings, felt her deadened limbs and body collapse into unconsciousness.

Her final thought, though: she would go looking for work, in the morning.